Eve Adams was born in Epsom, Surrey
and 'A Mixed Bouquet'
is her fourth book.
Married with two sons, she is a
lifelong fan of rock 'n' roll music.
Her favourite authors are
Robert Ludlum and Edward Rutherfurd.

A MIXED BOUQUET

BY
EVE ADAMS

Hope all goes well for you, Best wishes from Eve Adams December 3 2024

EV BOOKS

This is a work of fiction. Names, characters, places and incidents are either the product of the author's imagination or are used fictitiously.

Published and Distributed by E. V. Books
3 Canada Road, Byfleet, Surrey KT14 7JL.

FIRST EDITION

First Published February 2001

© by E. V. Books 2001
© Cover Illustration by T K Spencer

ISBN 0-9538369-3-2

Set in Times 11 on 12pt.
Design and Typesetting by
T K Art & Design, Addlestone, Surrey.

Printed in Great Britain by
Woking Print & Publicity
Woking, Surrey.

For David, with my grateful thanks for all your help and advice.

CONTENTS

GIRLS' NIGHT OUT

She was about to step into the foaming bubble bath, enjoying being on her own for the first time in ages. Her husband was out for the evening at a business dinner, and her sons had gone out with their friends. As she dipped her foot into the heavenly warmth of the bath, looking forward to the chance of pampering herself for a while, the phone rang.

'Damn!' she said. 'How *do* they know?' Sighing to herself she picked up the receiver. Before she could speak a breathless voice at the other end said: 'I've locked myself out! I've got Reg coming round for dinner and I was just going to the off-licence for a bottle of wine. I picked up the wrong keys, the neighbours are out, and I need to climb in through the bedroom window; it's the only one I left open!'

She stifled a groan. 'It's O.K.' she said, 'I'll be there in 10 minutes.' Brushing aside the 'thank-you's' pouring down the phone, she quickly threw on her jeans and trainers, grabbing a shirt from the chair and running down the stairs to pick up her jacket as she headed for the front door.

Trust Flo! Only she could do this. Lulu quickly locked the front door behind her as the sleek body of the fluffy black cat hurtled towards the opening, sensing freedom. She winced as she heard the thud as the animal smacked into the closed door, apologising to him through the letterbox.

It was cold outside. 9 o'clock on a dark winter's night, and here she was on an errand of mercy instead of soaking in the luxurious bubble bath. Oh well, what are friends for?

Racing through the dark country lanes, she arrived at Flo's house to find her standing shivering in the driveway. Her car keys were on the same key ring as the house keys, sitting smugly on the table in the hall. The open window was at the back of the house, above the conservatory. The two women picked their way carefully around the garden path in complete darkness, giggling together as only good friends can at times like this.

Usually to be found wearing trousers, Flo had tonight decided to dress up for her new beau. Lulu took in the tight mini skirt and low-cut blouse with a raised eyebrow. It was freezing out here, and Flo's teeth chattered as she lugged the ladder into position against the conservatory wall. Trying not to laugh, Lulu watched her good friend attempt to climb the ladder in her 3″ stiletto heels, knees clamped together by the tightness of the tiny skirt.

It was doomed to failure. Not only could Flo not lift her leg high enough to get onto the roof, the dip in temperature had created the equivalent of an ice rink on the sloping glass. Slipping and sliding, Flo looked down at Lulu to check what kind of footwear she had on.

They decided that it might be safer to swap shoes. Back down on the ground, Flo slipped off her high heels and exchanged them for Lulu's white trainers. The incongruity of the short skirt, black tights and white trainers made them both giggle. 'Like something out of St. Trinian's,' said Lulu, as hysteria began to set in.

Once more Flo started up the ladder, leaving Lulu dressed in jeans and high-heeled shoes over her white socks. At the top of the ladder Flo swung her leg as far as she could onto the icy roof. 'Gawd!' thought Lulu. 'Talk about the Grand Canyon!' Trying not to look up into her friend's nether regions, she held tightly onto the ladder to stop it from slipping. She tried not to think of the welcoming hot bath awaiting her at home as she shivered in the freezing night air.

It was obvious that her relaxing evening at home had just been consigned to the scrapheap. Biting her lip to stop her teeth chattering, she concentrated on holding the ladder steady as Flo teetered on its topmost rung.

It was hopeless. Even with the trainers on Flo could not gain a foothold. The open window remained tantalisingly out of reach as the two women stared at each other, not knowing what to do next. Their laughter rang out into the still night as the pair of them collapsed in hysterics. Dressed as they were, and helpless with laughter, had anybody been in the vicinity they might well have been mistaken for a couple of escaped inmates from the local asylum.

Tottering back to Lulu's car to sit in the warmth, they decided that they had no choice but to ring either the police or the Fire Brigade. There were no small windows they could break, only large panes of glass, and Flo was adamant this was not an option. Emergency or not, she was not having her precious new windows smashed.

Shivering together as the car heater roared into life, and trying to maintain at least a modicum of decorum, they waited while the mobile phone operator connected them to the local police station.

As Flo recited their predicament to the poor officer on the front desk, Lulu tried valiantly to stifle her giggles. She failed dismally, and, kicking off the stiletto heels, she wriggled her toes in an attempt to get some warmth back into them as Flo chatted animatedly to the police officer. Lighting a cigarette as she spoke, Flo waved her hand at her friend, demanding a pen and paper. The police officer was giving her the phone number of a locksmith, which she had to write down. He would come out himself, the policeman kindly offered, but they were short-staffed that night and he could not leave the desk. He hoped the locksmith would be able to help.

As she said 'goodbye and thank-you' to the bemused officer, Flo checked the mobile and swore. 'Bloody call cost me six quid,' she muttered, 'and the police station's only at the end of the road!' Once more the two collapsed into hysterical giggles, and exchanging shoes in the cramped interior of the low-slung sports car, they decided that there was nothing for it but to contact the locksmith.

Another lengthy call established that a man would be sent out at once to rescue the damsels in distress. It would take him about twenty minutes to get there. By this time, all thoughts of the meal being ready when Flo's new man arrived had been dispensed with. They agreed that, while they waited, it would be extremely sensible to go and pick up the wine. At least they were now warm, despite Flo's lack of sensible clothing.

Disappearing into the off-licence, cigarette in hand, she was teetering dangerously on the high heels. Minutes later she reappeared, two plastic glasses in her hand, and two bottles of wine tucked under her arm, thoughtfully uncorked by the friendly proprietor. Still helpless with laughter, they drove back to the house to await the arrival of the promised locksmith.

In party mood now, they sat in the car with the heater blasting away, drinking the wine and enjoying a cigarette or six while they swapped saucy stories.

Flo's mobile rang. It was her date, running late. Trying to sound coherent as the wine took hold, she explained what had happened as best she could. Nothing she said made much sense, and the poor man on the other end of the phone became increasingly disconcerted by the slurred utterances issuing from the receiver.

As a white van with a flashing yellow light on its roof arrived at the gate, Flo hastily said her goodbyes and

4

switched off the phone. Struggling out of the low car, her skirt now only just covering her backside, and the wine hitting home on an empty stomach, she lurched towards the young driver with bottle and glass held out towards him.

Her first words, 'Would you like a drink?' caused him to falter in his advance up the path. Faced with a tottering woman in high heels, bottle in one hand, cigarette in the other and wearing a skirt like a pelmet, he reacted with admirable aplomb. Gallantly brushing aside the offer of a glass of wine, he allowed her to lead him to the front door to inspect the lock, peering back over his shoulder at the shadowy figure in the car he could just make out through the darkness.

Inside the car a helpless Lulu was rolling about in fits of giggles. The sight of her friend clinging onto the hapless young man as she desperately tried to pronounce her words without slurring was just too much. She clutched her stomach as the locksmith tried out the keys he had brought with him while Flo stood gently swaying behind him, knees knocking with cold but bravely determined to help him if she could.

Through the windscreen, Lulu could see his hands trembling as he fumbled with the keys, and she knew that it was not just the cold that was causing it. The poor devil had only just arrived, but he was already more than a little unnerved by a tiddly Flo and the sound of inane laughter coming from inside the car.

With his special headgear on, a light on each side of the helmet, the young man looked like something out of 'Alien' as he struggled in the darkness, keys jangling like a prison warder's. Once again the two women, exchanging glances through the car windscreen, were losing the battle to keep control of their mirth. As Flo continued to refill her glass and empty it in record time, Lulu got out of the car to replenish her own glass. Flo was combining chain-smoking with unceasing chatter, and the locksmith was fighting to keep his panic under control as the lock refused to budge.

In the freezing night air the unlikely trio congregated around the front door, the poor young man now totally unnerved by the two tipsy, giggling women. As his hands trembled violently, key after key was rejected. He had decided, after a quick inspection, that he would not attempt the ascent to the open window over the icy conservatory roof, and it was now solely up to him to find a way to unlock the front door. The weight of this knowledge was obviously hard for him to bear, in his current surreal situation.

As the minutes ticked by and the lock remained stubbornly unpicked, the freezing friends adjourned once more to the car. Cursing under his breath, their would-be rescuer tried every key on the chain again, increasingly desperate now to get the door open and escape from these two crazy women.

With the wine and the cigarettes to keep them happy, they watched through the windscreen as the locksmith finally gave up the struggle to find a key that worked, and resorted to fetching a drill from the van. Progressively the two friends slid further into wine-induced euphoria, totally unable to stop giggling at the absurdity of the whole situation.

The piercing whine of the drill echoed suddenly into the still night, unleashing fresh gales of laughter from the two women in the car. Flo popped in and out to check on the young man's progress, each time taking longer to struggle out of the car. Her high heels clacked on the path as she tried not to stagger, but it was useless.

The young man kept his nerve only with a tremendous effort as the tipsy and increasingly tactile Flo leaned up against him on the pretext of checking on his success or otherwise with the stubborn lock. His entire body was shaking now as he struggled manfully to maintain his grip on his shattered nerves.

When at last the poor man succeeded in drilling through the lock and opening the door, two dribbling wrecks stumbled past him into the warm house, leaving him gaping on the doorstep. He stood no chance! Before he could collect his wits and make a run for it, Lulu turned back and grabbed his arm, dragging him into the hallway. His look of panic, etched so clearly on his face, simply led to Flo putting her arms around him in a gesture of thanks, thoroughly terrifying the poor devil. Pulling him through into the kitchen, despite all his efforts to the contrary, the women set to work to get the evening back on track.

Trying desperately to hold onto reality, Flo gamely gripped the worktop to keep herself upright as the young man wrote out an invoice with a shaking hand. Parrying constant saucy remarks from Lulu, he managed somehow to drink a cup of tea while he hastily changed the offending lock and gave Flo two new keys. She teetered around the kitchen putting potatoes into the oven, making gravy and generally attempting to continue with the preparation of the evening meal as though nothing had happened. Her incessant, rambling chatter did nothing to alleviate the young man's discomfort.

Oblivious to everything now except the completion of her beloved's supper, Flo stumbled from cupboard to cupboard, banging plates, glasses and cutlery down onto the work surfaces. Her attempts to bend over far enough to reach into the low Aga oven were enough to bring beads of sweat to the forehead of the unfortunate young man, standing in the middle of the room looking for all the world like a condemned convict one step away from his execution.

Desperate to get away from this crazy place, the young

locksmith was bombarded with more tea and biscuits, the women refusing to let him out into the freezing night without some sustenance to keep him going. Surrey's answer to Thelma and Louise had the poor soul in a pincer movement, from which there was no escape. His sole ambition in life now was to make a quick getaway, and his lips moved soundlessly in a silent prayer for celestial help.

A second call on Flo's mobile from her Reg somehow persuaded him that things were absolutely fine, as the poor deluded man decided to continue his journey to visit her. Had he been able to see what was happening in the kitchen at that very moment, he would undoubtedly have turned the car around and headed for home.

Blocking the young locksmith's retreat by lolling against the doorpost, Lulu decided that she needed a sandwich before she drove home. Wine alone was not conducive to safe driving, and between them they eventually managed to locate the bread, butter, sliced beef and pickle. Wielding a knife like someone out of 'Psycho', Lulu concocted a hideous-looking doorstep sandwich. Offering the locksmith a bite, which was hastily refused, Lulu gobbled the food in the hope of soaking up at least some of the alcohol, bringing on an immediate vicious attack of hiccups.

She slid daintily onto the floor as the combination of wine, giggles and loud hiccups turned her legs to jelly, and as the noise echoed around the kitchen, the young man was finally able to beat a hasty retreat as the two women yet again collapsed into uncontrollable laughter. One on the floor and one draped over the kitchen units in their mirth, the friends were crying with laughter and totally oblivious to the locksmith's escape.

As he shot out of the door in the search for some kind of normality, the young man almost cannoned into Reg, emerging from the darkness. Temporarily blinded by the two lights on the locksmith's helmet, Reg missed his footing and fell sideways into the flower bed. Not even glancing back over his shoulder at the felled newcomer, the locksmith hurtled on down the driveway to the safety of his van, breaking the world record for the hundred metre dash.

Dragging himself slowly up out of the frozen mud, and brushing forlornly at his dirty coat and trousers, Reg blinked rapidly as he tried to gather his wits. Mumbling plaintively about not being able to get his car into the driveway, the poor man surveyed the scene which greeted him. Two giggling, tipsy women stood barring his path, Lulu telling him to, 'Bugger off!' as she shut the door on him.

Out in the road the white van revved up and shot away from the kerb, wheels spinning, the driver desperate to distance himself from the madhouse. Poor Reg was at last allowed in through the door, understandably hesitant as he stepped inside the warm hall, and Lulu announced that she must leave to wend her way home. The two friends hugged each other, and tried hard not to dissolve into spasms of laughter yet again. It was not easy; it had been a mad evening.

Saying her goodbyes and scattering hugs and kisses all round, Lulu happily left the two lovebirds to their romantic – and very, very late – roast beef dinner.

Just after midnight, Lulu's husband received a phone call. He had just got in from his business dinner, and was disturbed to find his wife was not at home. Down the phone line came a familiar giggle, as she twittered at her bemused spouse in a loud and very slurred voice, interrupted by occasional hiccups.

'Hello dear. I'm in a prison cell. Been arrested by a very nice young occifer. Bit tiddly, don't you know?

How was *your* evening...?'

Before he could answer, another fit of giggling echoed down the phone and the line went dead.

'Oh God,' he said in dismay, staring at the receiver. 'What on earth has the daft cow done now?'

EXCHANGE OF CONTRACTS

They all sat round the log fire in the pub laughing and chatting, so pleased to be together again after all this time. It was 25 years since they had formed the band and had such a great time playing rock 'n' roll all over the world. Those had been the glory days, and the singer looked fondly around at the men she loved above all others. All in their 50's now, they had remained good friends over the years.

This was a rare occasion. The guys met up from time to time, but she had not seen them all for years. When the band had split up in the late 70's, she had moved into business in the City. The two guitarists and the drummer had all gone their separate ways.

Two of them had been deeply enmeshed in the era's drugs scene, and had been through the rehabilitation process during the last years of the 1980's. They were counsellors now themselves, helping others to escape from the nightmare world of drugs and alcohol.

Although music still played a large part in their lives, none of them played full time these days. An occasional gig; an evening in a wine bar now and then, just for the enjoyment, for their love of music.

They were all Londoners, she herself coming from the tough world of the East End. Her powerful voice had led her out of that environment and into the music industry. From her early beginnings as a pub act she had moved on to become a session singer. That was where she had met the others, all superb musicians in their own right. The idea to form the band had been put forward by the drummer, and things had progressed from there.

After months of rehearsals they had cut a demo disc and sent it out to the music giants. EMI had signed them up, and they had found themselves a manager to handle the bookings that began to come in. He was already promoting a number of bands and singers, and had found them a lot of venues over the years.

They had been so young and eager, their combined talents moulding themselves into a polished act very quickly. Sharing the song-writing, bit by bit they had begun to establish themselves in the business.

As their following grew they had a number of minor hits, culminating in a No.1 in Germany. They had toured the States and Australia, enjoying to the full their time in the spotlight. They seemed to have a golden future ahead, but little by little their personal lives had begun to pull the close-knit group apart.

As the drugs began to take their toll on the two band members, arguments had intensified and the pressures of touring and playing to packed houses increased. Petty jealousies and sheer exhaustion began to wear them all down. What had once been so much fun became a chore.

The singer sadly watched as the band began to disintegrate – missed gigs, continual in-fighting, and the downward spiral of the drink-and-drugs scene. Finally, they had begun to lose heart in themselves as a unit, and the touring ground to a halt.

Their manager seemed to have little interest in them any more. He was signing more and more new groups, and they were sliding in popularity. The singer knew that the writing was on the wall. Much as she had loved being with them, it broke her heart to see two of her best friends slipping into ill-health from their addictions. There were many tears and rows in those days, and their manager stopped promoting the band altogether as the rift widened.

The day they had the final meeting in his office was etched on all their memories. Sitting in front of the fire together on this December day, they relived that awful time. He had called them in for a showdown. They had no work lined up and no future; the next generation of groups was taking over the music industry.

He had told them that they were finished. He was dropping them in favour of his new signings. They had argued and pleaded for ages, but he was adamant – they were out. Nothing they said had any effect on his decision. There was absolutely nothing they could do, the man was too powerful. It was over.

Then he had dropped the bombshell. The band members had tried to discuss money, but he had simply handed them each a copy of the contracts they had signed five years previously. He took great pleasure in pointing out that, in the small print, was a clause which gave him the copyright to every song they had written over the years. They had been so eager to sign up with him, trusting him implicitly, that none of them had noticed that their work would belong to him in the future.

Morally corrupt it might have been, but it was legal. They could do nothing about it now. The meeting had ended in total chaos, threats flying from both sides. The drummer had promised to put a contract out on him, and the lead guitarist had to be physically restrained from beating the promoter to a pulp. They were manhandled out of the office by two of his security guards and, their world in ruins, they had adjourned to the nearest pub.

Back in the same pub now after almost 20 years, they could all remember it as though it were yesterday. The anger still burned deep, the sense of outrage remained undiminished.

Not a penny in royalties had they seen over the years.

Occasionally one of their tracks appeared in the charts somewhere in the world as it was re-released, but none of the band members received what should rightfully have been theirs. They had created so many songs between them, but the fat crook they had trusted lived the good life on their money. They were not the only ones – it was not just them he had treated so badly.

Down the years they had met many others he had cheated in the same way, but he was too rich and powerful to fight. He had known that none of them could ever afford to take him to court. Besides, they had signed their music over to him quite legally in their earlier naivety, too trusting to question this great man.

And he had taken full advantage of their innocence of the business world – he was an unscrupulous crook, but they had not known it then. They had learned the hard way, and it had cost them dearly.

Mature family men now, the musicians had tried to find ways to recover their lost copyrights and finances, but to no avail. Only the singer had turned her back completely on the music world to set up her own company. She had cut her losses and never looked back. Their manager's treachery had caused so much pain over the years, but it was a fait accompli. They had had to resign themselves to the loss of their songs.

The final insult had come only recently when a film had been released with one of their original songs on the soundtrack. That had hurt – they would not see any of the new money generated by this movie; it would all go to their ex-manager. Another stab in the back, but again, there was nothing they could do except enjoy hearing their music in a new and successful film. The old wound had been re-opened, however, and their frustration and anger had resurfaced.

Maturity had won the day though, and after much discussion and lively debate, the musicians shrugged their shoulders and went back to their families, ruing the day they had set eyes on their ex-manager. The drummer raised a few smiles as they all sat by the fireside, by wishing fervently that he had put that contract out on the evil bastard years ago!

The singer happily kissed the men who had been such long-term friends, and they parted company on that dreary winter's day after a magical few hours together. They all led different lives now. She ran her own very successful head-hunting agency in the City, and had promised to meet up with them again in the New Year. It had been a wonderful reunion; they must do it again very soon.

On New Year's Eve, the object of their mutual loathing lay soaking in his bath in a luxury hotel in Knightsbridge. He was fat and bald these days, but very, very wealthy. He awaited the arrival of his favourite call-girl from the agency. They would enjoy a sumptuous meal in his suite, and see in the New Year with her pandering to his every perverted sexual craving. She was good; the best. He could afford the best of everything these days.

He lay back in the warm water smiling in anticipation, his fat fingers holding one of Cuba's finest cigars, a bottle of chilled Bollinger on the floor within easy reach.

There was a knock on the door. 'Room service,' he thought. He was expecting it. He had left the door unlocked, and called out for the waiter to come in. He heard the trolley being pushed into the suite and reached out for his wallet. He always gave good tips; he was known for it. After all, he smirked, he could afford it.

He heard the bathroom door open and turned to see an elderly waiter standing there. He beckoned him forward and held out a £20 note to him. As the old man reverently shuffled towards the obese promoter wallowing in the bath, the fat man returned to his cigar and glass of champagne. The note was taken gently from his outstretched fingers, but he was aware that the waiter was still standing in the bathroom.

Remaining submerged in the water, he turned his head impatiently to see what the old man wanted. He froze, his eyes widening in terror and his heart beginning to pound. All he could see was the hand holding the gun close to his head.

Before he could move or cry out there was a muffled shot from the silenced barrel. Slowly, the disgusting bloated body slid down under the water, a neat hole in the centre of his forehead.

The elderly waiter lowered his arm and straightened up. Putting the small gun into his pocket, he turned on his heel and walked rapidly out of the bathroom, heading for the double doors to the suite. He reached the corridor, closing the doors behind him, and ran swiftly down the stairs to the floor below, his speed impressive for such an old man.

Taking out a key from his inside pocket, he opened the door and went inside one of the luxurious rooms, crossing quickly to the dressing table. Sitting down in front of the mirror he took off the grey wig and moustache, and removed the hotel's uniform jacket.

Shaking out her own silver-blonde hair, the singer grinned at her reflection in the mirror. She was good at this – all the stage costumes and make-up over the years had been good practice. She slipped the small gun into her make-up case, and covered it with an assortment of bottles and jars, to be disposed of later by her gangland friends.

After the disaster with the group, she had gone back to her roots and set up a bona fide company in the City with some of her friends from the East End. It was a double-edged sword; under cover of the legitimate head-hunting agency, the businessmen carried out their nefarious and extremely profitable underworld dealings, while she ran a highly successful and totally above-board company.

Fully aware of the dubious nature of her friends' worldwide interests, she kept her side of the business well away from any possible backlash, but so far it had been a tremendous success for both parties.

She had drawn the line at drug dealing though; she would not allow them to be involved in that. They must have no part in it. That was her only condition, the sole proviso within the company. She had watched too many friends suffer over the years, and she demanded their total adherence to this one unbreakable rule.

They respected her wishes; no drugs. She was a hard-headed business woman, and they made a lot of money using her agency as cover.

After her meeting with the band members a few days before, she had asked the East End mobsters for their advice on how to deal with the despicable crook who had caused them all so much trouble over the years. They had been succinct in their reply.

'Carry out the drummer's threat! Take out a contract on him.' With all their contacts, it would be easy to arrange. They offered her their help and their expertise. They would be pleased to exterminate the vermin for her.

'Even better,' she had told them. 'Let me do it. Let *me* pay him back for all the misery he's caused, the people he's ruined. For my friends.' At first they had tried to dissuade her, but her mind was made up. They could not shake her determination – retribution was to be hers and hers alone.

They had used their contacts in the hotel to set it up. Everything had been arranged for her. She had been taught how to use the small pistol so that it would look like a professional hit.

Despite their continued offers to carry out the killing on her behalf, she remained adamant. She had no qualms; the man had wrecked so many lives over the years, she knew she could carry it through. The thought of the despair and ruination he had brought to her friends in the band would be enough. She could do it. She would take revenge on the evil bastard – for all of them.

She stared back at the face in the hotel mirror, amazed at how calm she was feeling. The greedy fat man was dead, and good riddance. She had actually enjoyed seeing the terror on his face, and in the end, it had been so easy. She hoped that, with his death, the copyright issue could be resolved. That would be for her high-powered lawyer friends to sort out; she would get them on the case as soon as his body was found.

She had simply started the ball rolling; now time would tell. She had no doubt that everything would work out for the musicians, and that their songs would be returned to them after so many years.

Smiling at her evening's work, she looked at her watch – twenty minutes to midnight. Time to change and celebrate the arrival of the New Year. The party would be in full swing down in the magnificent Ballroom. She must hurry.

The singer thought of her friends, of the difference the death of such a nasty piece of work would make to their lives. He had screwed his last ounce of flesh out of the industry. He was history.

She had, quite simply, exchanged the manager's contract for one of her own.

Grinning happily, she stepped into the shower. She must be quick, join her friends to welcome in the New

Year. They would all be waiting for her, including the band members, as her guests.

'A very happy start to the New Year,' she thought as she stood under the warm water flowing over her. 'Health, wealth – definitely wealth! – and happiness.'

Stepping back into the bedroom wrapped in a fluffy white robe, the singer poured herself a glass of champagne from the magnum in the ice bucket on the table. Raising the crystal flute in a toast to the future, she formed the words in her mind.

To her special friends, her boys in the band – a very, very Happy New Year, filled with peace and prosperity. And a lot of money! Well overdue, but definitely a debt to be repaid.

Their old contracts had just been exchanged for new ones, courtesy of Nemesis. She smiled contentedly as she drank her champagne. They would never know the truth, but she did – and that was all that mattered. Judgment Day had finally arrived for the fat, greedy ex-promoter, and she was proud to have been the instrument of his downfall.

The singer stood and stared carefully at her reflection in the mirror. She still looked the same, despite what she had done tonight. Filled with a sense of inner peace, she began to dress for the party. It would be the best New Year's party ever for herself and her friends.

Revenge tasted sweet tonight – over 20 years late, perhaps, but still very, very sweet...

GUARDIAN ANGEL

She had drawn the short straw, there was absolutely no doubt about that. Being a Guardian Angel was not supposed to be easy, but good grief, there *were* limits!

She sat swinging her legs over the edge of the fluffy white cloud, her chin cupped in her hand as she gazed down at her young earthling lying peacefully asleep in his hospital bed, blissfully unaware of the previous night's events. The Casualty team at the local hospital had cleaned him up and cleared him out after his evening's celebrations had ended spectacularly with him tripping over his own feet and toppling into the river.

Polluted and smelly, the River Tyne was thick with slime and sludge from the ships and boats passing along it every day. The stupid boy had swallowed some of the putrid water before passing out in the slow-moving current. Luckily for him, the River Police had quickly hauled him out and packed him off to the medics.

It was, after all, the middle of November. Not exactly the perfect time of year for a midnight dip, especially in such foul water. 'Only my Tim could do this,' his rather bedraggled Guardian Angel was thinking to herself as she kept watch over his sleeping form in the narrow hospital bed. Only *he* could be so clumsy and such a headache to his minder.

He was *such* a trial to her. 'Enough to make a saint swear,' she thought, her tiny mouth turned down at the corners. Her halo was slightly askew and needed a good polish, and her slightly less than snow-white wings were drooping. All this worry; never-ending it seemed to her. Even now that he was grown-up, he continued to cause her everlasting headaches.

Sighing to herself as she watched over the troublesome young man, she realised that she was not looking as neat and tidy as an Angel should, but it was not her fault. Definitely not. She knew exactly where to place the blame for that.

When she had been delegated to keep an eye on young Tim, little did anyone realise just what a difficult full-time job it would be. He was a little devil, that was for sure. Always in trouble, and forever needing her guiding hand. No wonder she was worn out. None of the other Guardians, as they were known amongst themselves, had anywhere near as many problems with their earthly folk as she did with her Tim.

Despite herself, she did have to admit that he was a lovely lad really, just coming up to his 18th birthday. How he had managed to make double figures at all was a miracle in itself. Now he had discovered lager and women, big time! As a college student, he was dedicating himself one hundred percent to enjoying every minute of his life, and she was exhausted just trying to keep him out of trouble.

From the second he had got on his feet as a toddler, he had gone through life like a bull in a china shop; an accident waiting to happen. Sometimes, she could have sworn, he didn't actually have to *do* anything. Life just took hold of him and off he went again on another madcap spree, creating havoc wherever he went. Like a great big puppy, boisterous and noisy, he was a human whirlwind, scooping everything up as he hurtled through his allotted span.

Blond curls and sparkling blue eyes gave him the look of an angel, everyone said. Hah! Little did *they* know! This particular Angel was looking decidedly frazzled at the moment. Tired and constantly on watch, she was not taking enough care of her appearance – there just wasn't enough time with her frenetic, restless charge around.

Luckily, she did not need that much sleep, but keeping an eye on young Tim kept her on her toes night and day. How he found the time and energy to initiate such bedlam, she had absolutely no idea. If he was not asleep or more than a teensy bit tipsy, he was hurtling about the place like a lunatic; never still, always on the move.

If she tried to sit down quietly with a nice cup of celestial tea and a heavenly chocolate biscuit, he would need rescuing from some bit of bother as soon as she put her feet up, so she didn't even try that any more.

An extremely popular young man, he was always to be found in the company of lots of other youngsters out to enjoy life. Discos, pubs, nightclubs – on and on it went, night after night, with very little actual work being done at the college. No-one seemed to care, apart from his teachers, and they had given up on him a long time ago. He didn't notice. Nothing seemed to faze him as he cut a swathe through life.

She had to admit, though, she did quite enjoy the music and the dancing. She was obviously an Angelic Rocker. That was her favourite, rock 'n' roll, and she boogied on down to the beat, invisible to the world but having a whale of a time under the coloured lights. Halo at an angle, and wings beating in time to the music, she rocked along with the young dancers into the early hours of many a morning.

Her favourite trick at the discos was to hover in front of the purple light, which made her snow-white robe and wings shine even more radiantly bright. She giggled to herself as she shimmered and shook in time to the beat, almost wishing that these humans could see her, sparkling away there as she danced the nights away.

That, of course, had a lot to do with her being tired, she realised. After all, there probably weren't that many

Guardian Angels who went to discos most nights of the week. Add to that being on watch over young Tim 24 hours a day, and she really could not be expected to look spick and span, could she?

As she sat on her cloud, her little ankles crossed and her magnificent wings folded around her, she watched Tim smiling in his sleep and thought back over the years to the many times she had needed all her strength to cope with his antics. She lifted her arms and straightened her halo again as she remembered some of the things this lad of hers had got up to as he grew up.

Patting her long golden hair back into place and fluffing out her wings a little, the beautiful Angel wrinkled her tiny nose as she recalled how worried she had been about him, on so many occasions.

She had been in the police cell with him the night the local constabulary had found him wandering along the main street stark naked, loudly singing rude rugby songs. It had been her first visit to a prison in all the years she had been on Guardian duty, and she had not enjoyed the experience one little bit. It had been very smelly, dirty and noisy – and so had Master Tim, come to that!

She thought back over his madcap life; everyone said he lived a charmed existence. Nine lives, like a cat. That was, of course, entirely due to her help, otherwise Heaven alone knew what would have happened to young Tim. It would have helped enormously if she could know in advance what major problems lurked just around the corner, as forewarned is forearmed, of course. But then, Tim was quite capable of turning any molehill into a mountain all by himself.

Whether he was on roller-skates, a bicycle or a skateboard, the result had always been the same. Disaster! He just could not avoid hurting himself – it was simply a matter of time. There was no part of his anatomy he had not damaged in one way or another over the years. He loved sport, but seemed unable to play any game without sustaining an injury or two. Many a time he had been taken off the pitch on a stretcher, and sent by ambulance to the local Casualty Department.

Tonight was even dafter than usual. He had tripped over his own feet this time, ending up in the freezing river. As he bobbed up and down in the filthy water, the Guardian had held him up by his hair until the River Police launch came alongside and hauled him in. She was invisible, of course, to humans so it was extremely lucky for Tim that she was always so close to him and could keep an eye on him.

She had been tempted on many an occasion to administer a celestial smack, but it was strictly forbidden, and she never broke the Guardian Rules.

His mischievous nature had created many problems over the years, too. He was always playing tricks on people, or being naughty enough to need a good telling-off.

She sighed again as she recalled how many times he had been in detention at school. She had been really fed up just sitting there until the bell went, twiddling her thumbs while he did the work that had been set for him.

Just when she thought that he had calmed down a little, off he went again. He had broken his leg falling off a wall when he was 12, just before going on holiday to Spain with his family. They had had a dreadful time keeping the little monkey out of the sand, she remembered. He had wanted to play on the beach and go swimming like all the other kids, but his plaster cast had prevented that, and the whole family ended up feeling sorry for him, and spent the holiday in their room playing board games with him.

'Goodness, if they had known what I knew,' she thought to herself. The way he had chased poor Ralphie the ginger tom along the orchard wall with a catapult before he finally slipped, fell off and broke his leg. 'Hmmm,' thought his Guardian Angel. 'The family would probably have locked him in the hotel room on his own, and handcuffed to the bed, if the truth had come out!'

Then there had been that dreadful occasion when he had set fire to his bedroom. Of all things, he and a friend had been trying to barbecue some ants with his Dad's cigarette lighter, and the curtains had gone up in flames. The Fire Brigade had quickly arrived to prevent too much damage, but the entire family had gone to Casualty that time after breathing in the smoke.

Even the Guardian had got her wings blackened around the edges, and had a cough for a week afterwards. And the trouble she had had to get her halo clean again! She shuddered at the memory.

In addition to his many sporting disasters, he had been to the Accident Department of the local hospital so many times they knew him personally, and he no longer had to book in. The Angel was used to spending hours hovering over a cubicle, making sure he was all right, checking the plaster cast on his wrist, ankle, or whichever bit he'd broken this time.

The hours they had spent in there, she could have painted the sky from end to end. Not that it needed doing really, but it would have made a nice change from loitering about in different emergency rooms waiting for her young nuisance to be patched up yet again.

She sighed to herself as she sat on her cloud, trying to fluff up her drooping wings a little more and watching Tim snore the night away in the small hospital bed. She crossed her tiny arms and frowned as she looked down upon the angelic face of the young man who caused her so much trouble.

He was very lucky, lying there peacefully asleep and

remembering nothing about his brush with death in the freezing waters of the murky river. Dare she risk a short nap while he was asleep? 'No,' she thought, 'definitely not – he's just likely to fall out of bed and break something.'

Over the years she felt that she had aged like the humans down below, although Angels are not supposed to change at all; forever young and beautiful. Well, none of the others had had to look after young Tim, had they? He really had been a nightmare to watch over, always in some kind of trouble. He would make any Angel look old in a very short space of time, she was sure.

The Guardian pushed her halo back up yet again as she kept her protective watch over the accident-prone young man, wishing that for once she could relax a little; snooze for a while, perhaps. But no... it was better to stay awake, just in case. She simply did not dare take her eyes off him for one minute.

Despite all the worry he had caused her, she had grown to love young Tim very dearly. The thing was, she knew a secret about her young man, something very few others knew. She had watched many times over the years as he had shown great kindness to sad or lonely people above and beyond the call of human duty. He had spent hours whilst in hospital on his many admissions, visiting other patients, and sitting chatting to sick men, women and children, bringing them comfort and laughter.

He had the knack of cheering people up; making them feel better however ill they were. He had a very special gift – he could bring light and laughter into people's lives; he could turn their misery into smiles. He was blessed with an ability to transform despair into hope, tears into laughter, and he used it when and wherever it was needed.

But she had watched him cry for these people, too, his

heart heavy, when he was alone in his room. He cared, he really cared, for them. It was such a lovely part of his nature; it made up for all the difficult times.

His capacity for love was unlimited; he was a very special human being. At those times when she could cheerfully wring his neck herself – an extremely *un-angelic* trait, she admitted to herself – it was his wonderful ability to make others feel loved and cared for that rose above all else. It made her realise that he was, after all, well worth protecting.

Her drifting thoughts returned to his current sorry state, and she looked down once more on her young man. He'd gone! *Now* where was he? She flew quickly down to hover above his empty bed. She looked to left and right. Where had the little devil disappeared to? Now what was he up to?

He had been fast asleep, safe and sound! The Guardian began to panic, flying quickly up and down the ward.

Then she heard low voices coming from behind the curtains drawn around a bed at the end of the ward. Slipping silently inside them, she found Tim in his hospital gown sitting on the bed, holding the hand of a very old man, obviously extremely ill. Tim's face shone with the compassion of a gentle, caring soul as he stroked the man's hand, talking quietly to him as he began his journey to a world free from pain and illness.

The old man was smiling up at his young visitor, a smile of total peace and happiness. His eyes were alight with the knowledge that he was not alone as his life drew to a close. His pain was forgotten as Tim sat whispering to him and holding his hand, bringing comfort and love to the frail old man in his hour of need.

As Tim bent his head gently towards the old man, the Guardian Angel felt a tear roll down her cheek. Little devil he may be, but her precious young earthling had the heart of an angel. She had, after all, done a good job in keeping an eye on him.

He made her so proud to be his Guardian, so very proud. All the mishaps, the problems and the accidents were as nothing at a special time like this.

The elderly patient laughed with delight as Tim gently stroked his thin, grey hair and told him a joke, the two of them enjoying these precious shared moments. The Angel could see how much this meant to such a sick person, and how he responded to the compassion and tenderness being shown to him by a caring young man.

He had been young once, too, and Tim reminded him of how he was, so very long ago. Forgetting his pain and his fear, he held tightly onto the hand of his strong, youthful companion, revelling in the joy of a happiness he had thought he would never feel again. His eyes were shining as he smiled up into the gentle face of the young man, his face aglow with a new-found peace and serenity.

The Guardian Angel smiled down on the scene, floating just above the bed, her heart full to bursting with love and pride as she watched her young charge bring such joy to the sick old man. Leaving them together in their new-found friendship, she spread her wings and flew silently upwards to her Heavenly home, her halo now straight and shining brightly. For now, all her worries were forgotten in these magical moments.

Glorying in the sheer delight of Tim's God-given gift of love, she sent a prayer of thanks winging its way to Him, together with a heartfelt apology for any doubts she may have had about her young earthling.

Whatever she had to do to help her Tim, she would do it. Hard work it would no doubt be, but he was worth it. She settled down on her cloud, her now pristine snow-white wings folded around her, and gave her halo another quick polish with her sleeve.

All was right with the world again. She continued to watch over the two men in the hospital ward, one young, one very old; sharing a wonderful new friendship which meant so much to them both.

Her face incandescent with her beautiful Angel smile, she relaxed at last, sure now beyond any doubt that Tim would live a long and happy life, with her help.

And despite himself!

HAIRLINE CRACK

No-one would notice, he was sure. It had been no more than a tiny split in the skin at the base of the skull, no bigger than a stray hair. Right on the hairline, too. Need a magnifying glass to spot it.

He looked coldly down at her lying sprawled on the floor, her head oozing blood onto the expensive carpet. Bloody nuisance, but nothing else he could do.

He was amazed at his lack of feeling, for had he not loved this woman for such a long time? And now she was dead.

It was her own fault. She shouldn't have told him about the other man. Only a kid. 25, for God's sake! What had she been thinking, cheating on him like that?

He bent over her again, checking the back of her head once more. Difficult to see now with all the blood, but when she had fallen and hit her head on the corner of the table the bleeding had started immediately. The skin was very thin there; it split easily. No-one would spot the original wound; it was minute, had hardly bled at all. He was totally confident. It would be assumed that death was due to her cracking her head open on the table as she fell.

Leaving her lying there he made his way to the bathroom. He carefully washed the blood off his hands and checked his clothes. Nothing – no stains, no tell-tale marks. He was clear. Walking back into the lounge he picked up the heavy brass candlestick and took it into the bathroom. Scrupulously he washed it with soap and water, using the nailbrush to remove any traces of blood there might have been.

30

Dried and polished it looked innocent enough, back on the mantelpiece with its twin. He sighed as he took in the scene one last time. She lay spread-eagled on the carpet in the ever-widening pool of blood. She was so beautiful, even in death. Why, oh why, had she cheated on him? What a waste. They could have been so happy together, like they had been at the start.

He let himself silently out of the back door and walked the side streets to where he always parked his car. They had agreed at the beginning – he must always leave the car in a different street and walk to the back door of the house. That way nobody would see him enter or leave.

As he put the key in the lock he noticed his hands were trembling. Finally the shock was beginning to set in. He slid into the driving seat and remained sitting in the darkness while he fought to bring himself back under control.

His thoughts returned to the evening's argument, and his hands continued to shake. He felt the nausea rising in his throat and struggled to regain his composure. She had asked for it, taunting him like that. They had been lovers for months. Her husband was in his 60's now and she had needed the extra excitement in her life. Everything had been going so well, then she had met this younger man. A bloody window cleaner apparently.

His fingers gripped the steering wheel as the nausea gave way to anger. How dare she! He had given her all the sex she needed, why the hell had she started her nonsense with another man? His hands were clammy with sweat as he relived the evening.

He had confronted her there in her living room. She had denied nothing; she was even proud of her behaviour. God, he had hated her then, listening to her boasting about their sexual exploits, telling him that he was too old for her now.

Something had snapped – he had lost control of his

temper and grabbed the candlestick, charging towards her like an enraged animal. She had raised her arm to fend off the blow, turning as she did so, and he had hit her on the back of her head. 'It was *her* fault,' he justified the mishit to himself, 'not mine at all. She deserved it, the bitch.'

As she had fallen to the carpet he had dropped the heavy brass candlestick, kneeling quickly by her side in total panic. He had acted instinctively, out of jealousy and fury, and now look what had happened. God, had he killed her? No. She was still breathing, albeit very shallowly.

He had begun to brush her hair off her face, then suddenly checked himself. Turning her head, he had peered closely under the hairline to see what the injury looked like. With his medical training he could see at once that it was just a tiny split in the skin, hardly noticeable, but probably with a skull fracture beneath it. He had hit her quite hard. Blood had begun to seep out of the wound, and she was deathly pale.

His mind working overtime, he had quickly weighed the pros and cons. If she regained consciousness she would tell the world that he had tried to kill her. And she would carry on her affair with that bloody window cleaner. He himself would be arrested for attempted murder, and no-one would believe a word he said in his defence.

An ageing ex-lover, usurped by a younger model. He could already picture the disbelief any statement from him would engender; the smirks, the innuendoes. He would stand no chance. It would be her word against his, and she would have the head wound to show the world. An X-ray would finish it, provide the damning evidence against him.

As the thoughts flashed through his mind, he swiftly made his decision. She must not be allowed to remember.

She must not destroy his life and his career.

She must not be allowed to recover.

The decision made, he had picked up her unconscious body from the carpet. Holding her carefully against him, he had moved her slightly nearer to the table, then cold-bloodedly let her fall again, angling her to ensure that the back of her head hit the corner. She had hit the table hard, already a dead weight. The blood had started flowing immediately, quickly spreading out over the carpet in a crimson pool.

Now he sat in the darkness of his car breathing heavily as the memory flashed through his mind. Nobody had seen him arrive, nor leave. No-one knew about their affair, he was sure, so he was quite safe. The tiny hairline wound caused by the candlestick was so fine it would be overlooked in any examination. The table edge had inflicted a much deeper gash.

There would be no further checks, he was totally convinced. That was quite obviously the cause of death, with the ensuing loss of blood.

Exhaling slowly, he began to relax as he started the car and pulled away from the kerb, heading for home.

He drove carefully, certain that there was absolutely nothing to link him to her death. He had not been to the house for a while before tonight, but now he knew that her new lover had. If there was anybody in the frame, it would be this younger man, not him. It was most likely that it would be accepted as an accident, but any doubt or suspicion would fall on the latest lover.

He was safe, absolutely no question about it. Pouring himself a couple of stiff drinks, the killer showered luxuriously under the hot running water until he felt he had cleansed himself of the evening's events, then went to bed and slept like a baby.

At 8 am the following morning, the pathologist entered

the city mortuary. Leaving his briefcase in his office, he donned his green smock and boots, then pushed through the heavy swing doors into the cold workroom of his professional world. On the stainless steel examination table lay the body of a slim and beautiful woman. He turned to his junior for the case details, and the student handed him the police report.

As he read through the minutiae contained therein, a Detective Inspector from the local police station entered the antiseptic atmosphere of the cold,white-tiled room. Well-known to all the staff at the mortuary, the middle-aged detective held out his hand towards the corpse on the table.

He looked haggard. 'This one's personal, Mike,' he said to the pathologist. 'We've been up all night. She's the wife of our old Superintendent; he only retired last year. Found her when he arrived home. Looks like she fainted and hit her head on the table as she fell. I know you always do a thorough job, but this one's special. We need a conclusive result, fast as you can.'

Mike Davies, the resident pathologist, nodded sadly and turned to begin his minutely-detailed examination of the body. He had worked with the retired officer many times in the past, and had shared many cases with him. It must have been a terrible shock for the old boy to find his wife like that.

He would produce his expert opinion as soon as he possibly could, but he would not rush this post-mortem. He was known for his total professionalism, and everyone respected his work. His reputation was second to none, and he was not about to race through an examination simply because he knew the dead woman's husband.

With the D.I. and his own junior watching closely, he worked quickly and thoroughly. His practised hands carried out the dissecting and weighing processes

34

expertly, and as he worked, he announced his findings into the overhead microphone suspended above the table.

He spent a long time checking out the deep wound at the back of her head. As his assistant took photographs at his request, he conferred with the C.I.D man. His initial examination was pretty conclusive, he told him, although he would double-check everything, of course. There was no doubt in his mind – death had been caused by the fall and the subsequent loss of blood from the head wound. Toxicology tests would be carried out, her blood checked for anything suspicious, and every possibility investigated.

However, it was obvious, even at this stage, that she would have been knocked unconscious immediately judging by the extent of the injury. It would be up to the police to establish how it had happened, but it would seem that this had been a sad and tragic accident. The combination of the massive loss of blood on top of the impact of the fall would have led to a swift death, if that was any consolation to her husband.

'Please convey my condolences to the Super, poor old sod,' Mike Davies said to the C.I.D. officer, patting him on the shoulder. The older man thanked him and turned to leave the room, shaking his head as he thought about how he could best tell his erstwhile boss about these preliminary findings.

As he reached the door he heard the young student call out excitedly, and turned to see him bending over the examination table. The pathologist himself walked back from the desk where he had begun feeding data into the computer, as his assistant began to talk animatedly.

Beckoning the two older men over to the head of the table, he held the dead woman's hair away from the large wound in the back of her skull. He had been in the process of cleaning up after the post-mortem when he had spotted something, and his excitement was palpable.

He was holding a strong magnifying glass in his hand, and, as the two men peered down through it to where the student was pointing, the C.I.D. officer drew in his breath sharply. There, under the brilliant arc lights set above the table and magnified through the glass, it was plain for all to see. The pathologist and the detective looked at the new discovery together while the assistant hopped from foot to foot in his excitement.

It was tiny; virtually unnoticeable, and finer than a piece of cotton. But it was there, just to the side of the extensive bruising around the deep gash. Minute, but definitely a second wound. Only the eagle-eyed student had spotted it, and the pathologist was forced to agree. He had somehow overlooked it, and there was absolutely no excuse for the oversight. He could not understand how he had missed it.

Congratulations were in order; it was excellent work on the youngster's part, and Mike Davies was mortified by his omission. He bent once more and examined the tiny mark with the magnifying glass. No doubt about it – there were two separate wounds. Now that the head had been cleaned up again, he could clearly see them both.

The police officer took out his notebook, his face showing his deep concern. Damn it, this opened up a completely different avenue of investigation. Two wounds to the head; the deeper one to draw their eyes away from the other, almost invisible, hairline crack, perhaps?

He sighed. This was not good news for his old boss. There would now have to be a full-blown inquiry into the death. Possible suspicious circumstances. He dreaded having to break the news to the old boy.

Whistling quietly to himself, the young pathology

student led the grim-faced detective out of the mortuary, pleased that he had noticed such an important detail overlooked by his oh-so-clever boss. The man was not infallible, after all. Smiling smugly, the lad went back to his work of cleaning up after the post-mortem, delighting in the knowledge that his discovery would be a big plus on any future C.V.

Beads of sweat had broken out on Mike Davies' forehead as he sat slumped in his office chair. How the hell did the kid spot that? His examination had been both thorough and professional, the initial findings conclusive.

Such a small detail, but it spoke volumes to the experienced police officer. It hinted at something other than an accident. Mike knew they would start digging now. No stone left unturned when it came to one of their own.

Damn the bloody student! The post-mortem had been difficult enough, for God's sake, working on her body. That agile, sensual body that had given him so much pleasure over the past few months.

He was so sure he had got away with it, covered his tracks, but no... Somehow he had managed to drop her on the table fractionally in the wrong place, the wound not quite covering the original tiny mark. The blood had spread so quickly, he had been too hasty in his assumption.

He banged his fist hard on the table as he realised what this would mean. They would not stop until they had the murderer, he knew that. It was a matter of pride.

Sitting now with his head cradled in his hands, the pathologist thought with dread of what would happen once they started delving into her past. They would be meticulous, unrelenting – they would do it for their old Superintendent. God, what a mess!

He was filled with panic at what the future would

bring. Cursing his luck, he sat alone in his office as the world closed in around him. His superbly analytical mind summarised the situation as he felt the sweat break out all over his body, and his stomach convulsed with fear.

One virtually invisible hairline crack, and one over-zealous student with a magnifying glass. That's all it had taken. The difference between an accident inquiry and a murder investigation.

Just how unlucky could he be?

NIGHT LIGHT

He was losing consciousness fast, he knew. It was freezing, and although it was imperative that he tried to stay awake, the battle was already lost. He lay pinned underneath his motorbike on the winding country road. It was 1 o'clock in the morning, pitch black apart from the starlit sky above him, and there was no possibility of anyone coming across him for hours. Very little traffic used this road because of the new by-pass.

His leg hurt like hell; he was sure it was broken – and the pain, God, the pain! He thought of Kate, his dear Kate, whose frantic phone call had sent him rushing out into the night two long hours ago. She would be waiting and worrying in the village. What would she do when he did not arrive?

She had been in a total panic when she called. The baby had started to arrive six weeks early and she wanted him there. Her voice, full of tears and fear, rang in his head as he struggled to stay awake. He had raced into the night on his big black Yamaha, forgetting his mobile phone in his haste. He had no means of calling anyone now, and he cursed his stupidity at his lack of thought.

He began to weep in frustration as the combination of cold and vicious pain tore through him. Kate was only seventeen; the love of his life. He had told her he would be with her at the birth of this child, and instead, here he was, trapped by his leg under his powerful, heavy bike, one step from oblivion. Likely to freeze to death out here in the wilds as the temperature continued to plummet.

He felt totally, utterly helpless and alone. Kate would be lost without him, he knew, and he felt his heart breaking as he remembered his promise to her. Throughout all their time together, he had never broken a promise. Now, when she needed him more than ever before, he was not there.

He cursed his luck, cursed the bike, cursed everything, but he knew he could not stay awake much longer. The darkness inside his head was spreading quickly and the temperature was dropping by the second. He was numb with cold and shock inside the thick, padded leathers, but nothing could dull the dreadful pain in his leg. The heavy bike lay where it had fallen, his leg underneath, and he could not move it.

He knew it was all his fault. In his haste to get to Kate he had been riding too fast, and the twisting road had become an ice rink as it froze. His thoughts had been on Kate and her imminent motherhood, and he had not concentrated hard enough as he hurtled through the night.

Only a short distance away from his precious girl, the bike had gone out of control on an icy bend, skidding sideways into the ditch and pinning his leg as it came to rest. The shock of the accident had passed as the minutes ticked by, to be replaced by fear and misery as the freezing night enveloped him in its icy tentacles.

Peering through the visor of his helmet, above him he could just focus on the night sky through his half-closed eyelids. Bright stars, brilliant in these clear, frosty early hours of the morning. He struggled to keep them in view, to stay focused on something, anything.

'Don't pass out,' he thought. 'For God's sake, don't let go! Think of Kate – beautiful, gentle Kate.' The tears came again as he pictured her lovely face in his mind, misting the inside of the visor and blurring his view of the world of ice surrounding him.

She was so young, and she had been so frightened. The

baby was coming too early, and he could hear her fear down the phone line. He had told her to keep calm; he would be with her shortly. And now look at him, trapped under the bike when he should be with Kate, helping her, supporting her. It was so unfair, and it was all his fault.

As he strained to keep his eyes open, watching the heavens above him, one of the stars seemed to be bigger than the others, and much brighter. It appeared to be moving too. 'Impossible,' he thought. 'A shooting star? A night light?' No, he must be seeing things, imagining it. Hallucinating, probably.

The rushing noise in his ears was getting louder, like a roaring sea in a storm, pressing on his eardrums, closing his senses down. He knew that he would inevitably pass out very soon; it was so difficult to fight against it. He was too cold, despite the thick leathers.

The light grew ever brighter, coming closer, and the throbbing in his head intensified. He was close to the limits of his endurance now, holding on to reality by a slender thread. Only the thought of Kate and the baby was keeping him sane, but he would give in to the encroaching blackness soon, he knew.

It was just too difficult to struggle any more, and his frustration was increased by the blame he was putting on himself.

'What a way to die!' His thoughts ran on, alone out here under his powerful motorbike, frozen together like a statue. Never to see his beloved Kate again, nor to hold the baby, the precious baby. Tears ran unchecked down his cheeks as he pictured the two of them in his mind; Kate and her child. His agony was intense, both emotional and physical as the mental image began to blur, and he felt himself slipping away.

At least he was not in total darkness now. Thank God for the stars; or was it the moon that was moving? He realised that he no longer really cared; he was beginning to give up the fight. It was impossible; he just wanted to go to sleep.

It was a struggle now even to keep his eyes open. He was so cold, his mind and body numb except for the gnawing pain in his leg. The light continued to shine brightly down on him, and he could see through his closing eyelids that he was bathed in a luminous glow as he lay there.

Maybe it was his Guardian Angel coming to take him away to join the Heavenly bikers! He grinned wryly at the thought, then finally losing the battle to stay awake, slipped away into deep unconsciousness.

There it was again, the bright light above him. He opened his eyes slowly, dimly aware that he was no longer cold. He could not focus properly, but he could hear voices, he was sure of that. Someone was holding his hand, and through the haze he could see people moving about. Where was he? His mind was trying to recall what had happened, but his head was muzzy, his brain like treacle.

Kate! Sweet Kate was here, smiling down at him. He could see her lovely face close to his. She was speaking to him. He could not believe it. She was here; his beloved girl, his adored Kate! No, it was not possible. He must be dreaming.

He struggled to get a grip on the situation, but she was stroking his head, telling him to lie still.

Was he dead? Was this all a figment of his imagination? A vision, perhaps? Fighting to keep his eyes open he tried again to look at this new world. Through the mist in front of his eyes he willed himself to concentrate, to see clearly, but surely his mind was playing tricks. None of this made any sense.

And who was this? A man in a white coat – a doctor, perhaps? Struggling hard now to comprehend, the unanswered questions crowding into his mind, he tried to think, to clear his brain. He must be in hospital then. But how? Where?

All too soon he felt himself sliding once more into the black abyss, the vision of his precious Kate fading as once more the darkness enveloped him.

His next awakening he would always remember, as he climbed slowly up out of the fog in his brain. Such a delight; an unexpected treasure.

He came to for the second time in his hospital bed, with Kate at his side and a nurse taking his temperature. As Kate's lovely face swam into vision, he made to hold out his hand to her, but before he could move, she kissed him on the forehead and told him to lie quietly.

Trying to speak, he found her finger on his lips, and, listening carefully as she told him what had happened, his concentration slowly began to return. He heard how, after she had telephoned him to say that the baby was coming, her brother Sam had arrived to see how she was, and had called an ambulance to the tiny cottage. It had brought her to the local hospital where she had been in labour for a long time.

When he had failed to arrive, Sam had informed the police that the biker had gone missing on his way to the cottage, and the emergency services had swung into immediate action. Because of the local terrain, the myriad country lanes and acres of farmland in the area, the police had sent up a helicopter in the hope of finding him.

The powerful searchlight beam from the aircraft had found him as it swept the countryside, and not a moment too soon. Hypothermia had set in, and he was in a bad way.

An ambulance had been dispatched to the scene of the accident, and had transferred him swiftly to the same hospital that Kate was in. It had been a close call, but the expert medical care in the Accident and Emergency Department had pulled him through.

'So that was it!' he smiled to himself. That was the bright light he had seen. Not a biker's angel after all, just the local police pilots. 'Angels of Mercy,' he thought as he momentarily relived his terror out there in that frozen landscape.

He gripped Kate's hand tightly, never wanting to let go again, and tried to speak, but she made him lie back on the crisp white pillows. The doctors had put his broken leg in plaster, she told him, and he could see that he was on a drip, but she reassured him that there was no serious damage. He would be a while recovering from his ordeal, but he was safe now.

Suddenly he remembered! He grabbed Kate's hand and whispered hoarsely and urgently. 'The baby, Kate, what about the baby?' She grinned down at him, her face alight with happiness, and turned away for a moment. Then he felt the tears prickle his eyes as a tiny white bundle was placed in his arms, a minute human being wrapped tightly in a soft blanket.

'Say hello to Jack, Dad. Your first grandson, you daft, lovable old biker, you.' His beloved daughter smiled down through her own tears of joy at the two most precious men in her life as the new grandfather gently stroked the baby's tiny perfect face, marvelling at the depth of emotion he was feeling for this newborn infant.

Cradling the sleeping child in his arms, he was totally unprepared for the overwhelming rush of love he felt for his daughter and her baby son.

He had been so close to losing them both. It was a miracle, nothing short of a miracle. 'Jack,' he whispered as he proudly looked down at the sleeping child. 'Jack.' His own name – handed down now to this tiny, perfect human being, his own precious grandson.

Through his tears, he watched the tiny mouth form into

a yawn as he held baby Jack close to his heart, his silent prayer of thanks winging its way into this special night of miracles.

BLACK WIDOW

Sheila dabbed her eyes with a tissue as she bade farewell to the last of the mourners. She had been surprised at the number of people who had come to John's funeral; so many more than she had expected. Of course, with a sudden death it is as much by word of mouth that people are informed as by newspaper announcements.

The past eight days had been very tiring, but today had gone as well as any such occasion can. The arrangements had worked to perfection, the service short but succinct, and everyone extending sympathy and kindness. The elderly vicar had known them both for many years, and his eulogy had moved many of the congregation to tears.

She closed the door feeling utterly exhausted, assuring her friends that she would be fine on her own, and wandered back into the sitting room where she sank down gratefully into the easy chair. Putting her feet up on the stool, she lay back and closed her eyes. As she thought back over the events of the past week, her hand reached out to touch the photograph of her and John on their wedding day, over twenty years ago.

She recalled how John had woken her in the middle of the night with chest pains, and how quickly the ambulance had arrived after her frantic 999 call. Then the nightmare journey to the hospital, siren wailing, as the paramedics had struggled in vain to save her husband.

The poor young doctor, so tired he could hardly stand, walking slowly down the corridor towards her; bringing her the awful news that her husband had not recovered consciousness and they had been unable to resuscitate him. Despite their very best efforts, they could not save him. The doctor was so very sorry, he said, his shoulders hunched as he passed on the dreadful news.

He was almost in tears, poor man, and Sheila had thanked him for all he and his team had done. She had told him that she knew they had done everything possible, and he was not to upset himself. John had a history of heart problems; he was not to blame himself, she had told the young medic.

It had been a dreadful night, one she would never forget. Alone in her loss, she had left the hospital and sadly returned home in a taxi to the empty house to collect her thoughts and her memories. It was at times like this that she regretted not having children, but she would have to cope, to get through this, on her own.

Old Dr. Matthews had been a tower of strength, calling in most days to check on her and prescribing sedation when necessary. He had reminded her of the weakness in John's heart diagnosed some years before; how his prescribed medication, Digoxin, was a powerful drug used to help people like John maintain a normal lifestyle by regulating the heartbeat. John had known he would have to be on this medication for life, but it was a small price to pay. It had enabled him to carry on as normal, working as an accountant.

Dr. Matthews had expressed surprise that John had had the heart attack when he did, as the Digoxin, a derivative of digitalis, had seemed to be steadying his heart quite satisfactorily. He had been to the surgery for regular check-ups, so it appeared to the good doctor that this was simply one of life's very sad occurrences.

Anything he could do, Sheila was to call him. He had patted her hand in a kindly manner, and she had sobbed quietly as he took the time to talk to her about her husband. He had always liked John, he told her, and he was so very, very sorry about his sudden, untimely death.

Sheila had been very grateful for his support and his help. She knew how busy he was, and it was extremely kind of him to be so caring and considerate.

The phone rang suddenly on the side table, waking Sheila from her doze with a start. As she moved to pick up the receiver her hand knocked over the photograph of her and John. As it crashed to the floor, the glass shattering on impact, she answered the insistent ringing with an impatient, 'Yes?' The voice in her ear soothed her immediately, and she settled back in the chair again with a smile on her face.

Dr. Ian Bolt, younger partner of Dr. Matthews, was enquiring after her health. She grinned. He was being a little saucy, considering she had just buried her husband!

Their conversation was short and to the point. In answer to his questions, she confirmed that the additional bottle of Digoxin tablets Ian had given her at their last meeting in the hotel had been thrown into the local river, gone for ever. No trace left of the extra pills she had been powdering into John's food, building slowly to the overdose which had finally triggered the massive heart attack.

Ian had assured her, as they went over the plan in great detail in their hotel room, that the increased intake of the drug would inevitably result in John's hastened death. His heart would be unable to cope with the extra dosage. Digoxin was a very powerful drug, and the dosage must be strictly adhered to. Any increase in the prescribed amount would inevitably lead to major problems, poisoning the system and unbalancing the heartbeat.

She had been very nervous at first, but Ian had assured her that there would be no need for a post-mortem, as

John had suffered with heart irregularities for years. It had been easy for him to access the records in the surgery and, as Dr. Matthews' partner, discussion of the case was also totally normal. He had no doubt at all that death would automatically be set down as the result of a massive heart attack after years of problems.

In short, there could be no easier way of removing Sheila's husband from the scene without suspicion, to allow the two lovers to continue their affair unhindered. She had been very careful with the extra pills, ensuring that her husband received the additional amounts slowly but steadily, building up to a poisonous overdose.

Crossing her ankles and stretching luxuriously in the chair, she put down the phone, a smile on her lips and joy in her heart. She could not wait to see Ian again, to feel his young body on hers. Such incredible passion and romance – so different from staid, boring old John. Still, he had never known about their affair and now he never would.

She had no qualms about what she had done, and no-one would ever suspect the truth. She and Ian had planned it all so carefully, and it had worked brilliantly. It was time she had some fun after all those boring years, looking after her dreary husband and keeping house.

She had fallen madly in love with the handsome young doctor, and she knew John would never agree to a divorce. So – there it was. 'Needs must when the Devil drives,' she thought – and Ian *was* a devil; a very, very sexy young devil.

Anyway, she looked good in black. She had played the grieving widow to perfection today, dressed in deepest mourning as befitted the occasion. Smartly-dressed in her grief, she saw her husband off in the best tradition, clothed from head to foot in black, even down to the tiny veil on her hat which did little to conceal her distraught features from a sympathetic world. That had been a nice touch, carefully thought out. A tiny black net veil to shield her face, but fine enough for everyone to see the constant tears she shed for her husband, and the grief-stricken face of loss. All part of the game.

In a short while she would be playing other games; sensual, erotic games, with her young lover. She wore black for him too, silk and lace, velvet or satin. Pretty, sexy undies that he had bought for her and she had kept hidden in her underwear drawer for their exciting meetings. Not that she ever kept them on for long, she smiled to herself as she relived their passionate visits to their favourite hotel.

They would have to wait a little while before they could meet in public, but until then their hotel room would provide the necessary seclusion from prying eyes. It was a large, anonymous hotel, very busy all the time, and far enough away from their home town to avoid any embarrassing meetings with anyone they knew.

Sheila stood the photograph back on the table, looking contemptuously down at the man she had so recently murdered. There was no feeling of guilt, no conscience at all. She got up from the chair, switching out the light as she left the room, and went upstairs to remove her mourning clothes.

She would have a long, soothing shower to wash away all traces of her alter ego, the mourning wife, the sad widow. 'Poor John,' they had said. 'And poor Sheila...'

Throwing her clothes onto the bed, she looked at herself in the mirror. Still pretty trim, despite the onset of middle-age, and still agile enough to enjoy a good romp with a younger man. She grinned as she thought of the future ahead with her handsome young doctor. She liked her new-found freedom. Perhaps, after all, it was just as well that she and John had no children. It could have complicated matters.

She liked the fact that everyone would be talking about her with such compassion at this sad time. There would be a few weeks of constant phone calls and visits while they made sure she was not becoming too depressed, but in time it would all calm down and she could return to some kind of normality.

In the meantime, she could look forward with delight to her clandestine meetings with her lover, made all the more exciting by the lies she would tell and excuses she would have to make to her friends. It added that extra bit of spice as she wove her tangled web of deceit.

Once everything had settled down, she could look forward to a new lease of life. Promising herself some happiness after the years of boredom with John, she stepped into the shower, without realising that she was humming one of his favourite pieces of music. With a sudden shriek of laughter, she recognised what it was – a tune from the operetta, 'The Merry Widow,' by Franz Lehar.

'Oh, what perfect irony!' she thought to herself as she stood smiling under the gushing water. Enjoying the sensual feeling of the warm water cascading over her body, she suddenly recalled what she had overheard earlier today at the funeral. She laughed out loud at the memory.

She could hear them now, huddled in a little group, unaware of her presence behind them. She shivered with delight as the words popped into her head. They were her passport to a whole new future.

'Poor Sheila,' they had whispered. 'Whatever will she do? How on earth will she cope, now that she's a widow?'

THE DRUMMER

She awoke with a start. Taking a minute or two to unscramble her brain she focused on the alarm clock. 3 a.m. 'Another restless night,' she thought.

What had woken her this time? As she turned over under the duvet she heard the unmistakable sound of her big black cat purring. Smiling, she reached down and stroked his furry head, tickling his ears and listening as the purring got louder. He loved to curl up against her on the bed, and she was grateful for his company.

She had not been sleeping well lately. It had been a hectic year; her eldest son had got married and moved away with his lovely young wife. And now her youngest son had flown off to New Zealand for a year with some of his friends, and the house was unnaturally still and quiet. The phone did not ring like before, and there were no hulking rugby players littering the kitchen and eating her out of house and home.

She had grown used to them being around, and she did not like the silence that pervaded the house now that the boys were not there for their friends to visit. Occasionally they would call or pop in to see her, but it was not the same.

The lads were taking a year off to see the world and play Southern hemisphere rugby, looking for jobs when they arrived in Auckland. It was a wonderful opportunity, but naturally their families were concerned for them while they were so far away; it was only to be expected. They were not the most shy and retiring young men in the world, either, and, apart from their rugby, they would undoubtedly leave their mark on the city of Auckland.

Their parents simply had to trust to luck and hope they would return home in one piece, having had a marvellous time.

Her son may be 24 and over six feet tall, but he was still her little boy, her youngest child. She would miss him so much, they all would, and worry about him until he got back home safe and sound. Social and sociable, he had brought a lot of happiness to the family, along with a multitude of sleepless nights wondering where he was, and what he was up to this time.

Unlike his elder brother, he was obviously going to take his time in settling down and getting a job. She was proud of her sons, and felt herself to be very blessed as far as her family was concerned. At times, when things got out of hand and a little too hectic, they would all have been grateful for a quieter life. But now that it was that way, she did not like it at all. It was too quiet, she thought.

It would be a while before she got used to him being on the other side of the world, and she knew the phone bill would be astronomic while he travelled to New Zealand and found somewhere to live for the year. As the boys had made their plans it had seemed like a dream, but now it was reality.

They were half a world away, and would be gone for a year at least. A year – it seemed an age to her as she thought back to the raucous farewell party such a short time ago.

Running her fingers through the cat's thick black fur, she lay quietly thinking about her son and his friends, now so far away from their homes and families.

Suddenly the cat sat bolt upright, ears pricked, eyes glowing large and luminous in the dim light from her bedside alarm clock. Alone in the big house she instantly came fully awake, aware of a noise somewhere downstairs.

What was it? She could not make it out at first, then her heart began to pound and her palms began to sweat as she recognised the sound of drumming, coming up from the basement. Her stomach tightened as the noise grew louder through the still night, unearthly but insistent.

She must be dreaming, she thought. The drum kit had stood untouched since her son had left for New Zealand. He was a superb drummer, playing with local groups after his music course in London. He was hoping to find a band to join out in Auckland, his love of music as strong as ever.

The cat shot off the bed to cower under the dressing table. She knew from his reaction that he too could hear the noise. She was not dreaming; she was wide awake. And someone... someone was playing the drums downstairs.

She was suddenly very afraid. The rhythmic beat echoed through the house, growing louder and louder in the silence of the night. Who was it down there? In her panic she fumbled for the phone, only to find there was no dialling tone. It was not unusual out here in the countryside. The phones did play up a lot, but why tonight, for God's sake, when she desperately needed to speak to someone?

Where was her mobile? Oh no! In the bloody car, she remembered, in the glove compartment. Damn it, she would have to go downstairs and out to the garage.

But she could not move; she was frozen with fear.

The volume of noise increased to such a pitch that it filled the whole house. She thought she would go mad. Through her terror the realisation filtered slowly that whoever it was down there was playing loudly but rhythmically – she could recognise what she was hearing. It made her shiver. It sounded as though her son was playing his drums, just as he had done so often in the past.

Switching on all the lights, she stood at the top of the stairs, her legs like jelly and her heart pounding in her chest. On and on went the drumbeat, cymbals clashing too. Swaying, she grabbed hold of the banister to steady herself.

Trying to breathe deeply and calm her fright, she started slowly down the stairs, knowing that she must reach the front door and open the garage to retrieve her mobile from the car. How stupid of her to leave it there.

God, but she was scared. She could hardly move, she was trembling so much, but she pushed herself on down the stairs as the noise from the drums echoed all around her, making her whimper with fright.

Of all nights, why tonight? She was not alone very often, so why was this happening now? Fear drove her on, down the stairs and towards the door, the drums filling the whole house with their unceasing beat.

She would drive away from the house so fast, using her mobile phone as she went. Call 999. Call her eldest son and his wife. Call anyone... just get away as quickly as possible from this nightmare.

Her husband was abroad on business; she could not phone him, could not reach him. Alone with her fear, the drumming was driving her mad as she forced herself down the last few stairs, her hands over her ears as she tried to block out the noise.

The house stood by itself near the village, surrounded by open farmland. There were no near neighbours she could run to. She had to get to the car. She had to get out of the house. She *had* to get away.

Incessantly the drums played on and on, tearing her nerves to shreds. As she stumbled down the last step and across the hall, desperate to pick up her car keys and sobbing with fright, she heard a sound that almost stopped her heart.

It was the cymbals – just the cymbals now. She heard

them through her terror and she stopped dead in her tracks.

It was the way her son used to play them. Right in the middle of a thumping rock number he would play a few bars just on the big golden discs, with his drumsticks.

It was his own personal signature; his own little composition. She loved to hear him play them like that, and he did it for her, for his Mum. Wherever he played, he would always tap out the little tune for her on the cymbals, and it had become very special over the years.

She stood, still rigid with fear, feeling vulnerable and isolated in the middle of the hall. But now, there was something else there too; she could sense something different, but she was still too frightened to recognise what it was. Beneath her feet the drumbeat started up again, but now the terror of the last few minutes was subsiding.

A quiet calm slowly began to take over from the fear, and her thoughts returned to normal as her mind regained its clarity.

As the drumming continued and the cymbals rang out, she turned away from the front door, her heartbeat settling down as the panic left her. She walked steadily into the kitchen, pausing only to switch on the lights.

Then, taking a few deep breaths, she opened the door to the basement.

As the neon strip lights flickered into life and flooded the room with suffused yellow light, the drumming stopped abruptly. She looked down onto the semi-circle of drums and cymbals standing there in the centre of the room. They were exactly as her son had left them. Waiting for him to return home. Waiting for him to play them again.

There was no-one here. Only the drums, polished and silent.

As tears began to cloud her eyes, she stood for a while

looking at his precious drum kit, reliving the many happy hours he and his brother had spent together down here. One son on guitar, one on the drums; their Dad adding a vocal or two from time to time. 'Wild Thing' was a particular favourite, played over and over again, and so many other rock 'n' roll songs had been done to death in this room. Even she had had a go, setting aside her embarrassment and letting rip into the microphone.

She smiled through her tears as she stood at the top of the basement stairs. She had watched her family enjoying their music with so much happiness, and a mother's pride. Once again she looked down on the silent drums, the cymbals motionless and shining brightly under the lights, and thought back to those happy days when they were all together.

Tonight was totally beyond her comprehension. What had happened here, she had absolutely no idea. It was a complete mystery, terrifying at first, but it had brought her son closer to her, his special tune on the cymbals reaching through her fear and calming her.

Somehow it had eased her concern about him, so far away. She knew instinctively that he was all right, and that the family's strong bond of love had reached out across the world in some strange but wonderful way.

No longer frightened, just puzzled and thoughtful, she took one last look at the drum kit and, turning back into the kitchen, switched off the basement light.

Twelve thousand miles away in Auckland, the tall young man sat at the table in the house he was sharing with four of his friends. Thinking about his family back home in England, he picked up a knife and a fork and, holding them like drumsticks, began to beat out his favourite rock song on the glasses and plates laid out on the table. He smiled as he thought of his drum kit standing in the middle of the basement at home, and of the hours he had spent there, jamming with his friends and family.

Glancing at the clock he realised that it was now the early hours of the morning in England. 'They'll all be asleep,' he thought, as he rapped out his special little tune on the glasses, as he always did on the cymbals at home.

It was his signature, his own little composition. His Mum loved to hear him play it.

How he wished she could hear him now...

THE NIGHTMARE OF JESSE GAUNT

He awoke violently, abruptly. He was bathed in sweat, his mouth open ready to scream. The nightmare again, that damned nightmare! Every night, always the same.

Staring up into the darkness, he tried to calm his shaking limbs, fight the rising nausea. How many times did he have to go through this? What the hell was happening to him?

Jesse lay on the bunk bed, too scared to move, still in shock. He knew this would pass eventually, it always did. But why did he keep having this bad dream? Just what was triggering it?

His head was pounding, his limbs like lead. Dear God, what was going on here? Night after night, he had become scared to go to sleep. He knew the hellish nightmare would return. Time after time he had woken in terror, sweating and screaming, the bedclothes soaked with sweat where he had thrashed about in his torment.

Tonight was the worst so far. He lay as still as he could, taking stock of the situation, his heart still hammering inside his chest.

'Rationalise, Jesse. Take time and work through it. It's only a bad dream, nothing more. Get a grip on yourself, fight it.' Jumbled thoughts ran through his mind as he attempted to drag himself back to reality.

He tried to think calmly through the nightmare, but it was so horrible to relive. It always began with him in the condemned cell on Death Row. Which prison, he could not tell, but it was bleak, dark and forbidding. The scenario was engraved on his memory; he had been there so often over the last few weeks.

It appeared that he had murdered an elderly priest in the confines of a church, stabbing him to death, and the State Prosecutor had demanded the death penalty. The jury had found him guilty, and he had been sentenced to execution by lethal injection.

There was no recollection in the nightmare of any trial, nor of the crime for which he had been convicted. He was simply aware of the events and the fearful sentence passed on him.

His appeal had been turned down and the nightmare grew ever deeper as he waited in his cell on that final morning. That was always where the horror began – in the cell, awaiting execution. It was always the same. He knew there was no escape; he was going to die.

He struggled to wake himself up but his torture continued. He saw in his sleeping mind the prison Chaplain enter his cell to hear his confession. Jesse heard himself screaming through his terror, 'I didn't do it! I'm innocent! Help me God, please help me!'

The Chaplain nodded wisely and sadly as Jesse raged on, reading aloud from the Bible as the condemned man fought back tears of anger and frustration. He remained calm as Jesse threw himself about in his agony, restrained only by the shackles on his wrists and ankles.

He tossed and turned in his sleep as the nightmare deepened, crying aloud in his despair. Now the elderly Chaplain and two prison warders were walking with him towards the Execution Chamber. He dragged his shackled feet as the two burly guards held him up between them, fighting them all the way. He was terrified, struggling to escape, shouting that they had made a terrible mistake.

Jesse Gaunt was innocent! Why couldn't they hear him? Why wouldn't they believe him? He thrashed about on his bed as the nightmare enfolded him in its horror, making him watch his own terror over and over again.

He groaned in his misery as he watched them strap him down onto the hospital trolley, heavy leather restraints across his chest, hips, thighs, ankles and wrists, pinning him down. He tried to cry out, to wriggle free, but he was held tight. He could not move; he was paralysed by the heavy bindings.

Jesse saw the Chaplain and the warders leave the Chamber as the prison doctor moved slowly towards him. On the other side of the one-way glass partition he knew there was a small crowd of people – faceless people, there to witness his execution, all watching his agony in these last minutes. He tried to move on the trolley, screaming his innocence into the air, but the restraints held him tight in their unrelenting grip.

Beneath the bandages on his wrists were the tubes which would feed the poison into his veins at the appointed time. They led into one big plastic tube set in the wall of the chamber, and he knew that time was running out for Jesse Gaunt.

He saw himself strapped there so tightly, unable to help himself, yet fighting in his sleep to free himself from his fate. In vain he tried to wake up, but the nightmare continued unabated, as always.

He was cursing and swearing at the unseen watchers, surveying the scene with increasing terror as the prison doctor drew near. His pulse was taken, his heartbeat checked as he screamed his innocence into the echoing small chamber, then the doctor withdrew and left him alone in the final seconds of his life.

Now he could hear the distant voice of the Chaplain praying for him as the climax of his nightmare approached. Jesse screamed without a pause for breath, every sound captured by the overhead microphone placed there to record his final words. Agonisingly, his shouts of fear and terror reverberated around the chamber and into the tiny room where the onlookers stood, not one of them able to remain impassive in the presence of such utter despair.

Jesse kept on shouting his dreadful torment at the world as he tossed his head from side to side, waiting for the inevitable oblivion to overtake him.

Still he could not awake. Nothing could stop the nightmare. He was trapped inside its horror, on and on until it was ready to release him, as he knew it finally would. But not yet – not just yet.

Knowing what was about to happen, because it was always the same, once again he felt the poison enter his bloodstream, felt the immediate heaviness in his limbs, the nausea and the pounding blood in his body. One last eruption from his tortured lungs, and then – the awful darkness, pitch black all around him.

Not a glimmer of light. Total eclipse. Hell on Earth. This was the part of the nightmare where he always woke up screaming, bathed in sweat and heart hammering – like tonight. Again.

He stared up into the inky blackness above him, struggling to bring his body back under control. The bed was a mass of twisted sheets, soaked with sweat, as usual. His breathing began to slow and his heart rate decreased as he began to calm himself.

It was a horrific nightmare, recurring as it did on a nightly basis. He resolved to see a doctor about it soon. This was far too much to cope with; it was affecting his life, his health, and his sanity. It must be stopped – he would get it stopped, come Hell or high water.

He sat slowly up on the bed, switching on the overhead light with shaking fingers. He noticed at once how hot it was in his room. The cold sweat on his body from the terror of the nightmare was now warm, the room like a sauna. He was drenched from head to toe, and he was still trembling.

Wiping his forehead with the back of his hand, he resolved to get the air conditioning fixed as soon as possible. It was steam heat down here in the South at this time of year, hotter than Hell itself. First though, he needed a drink, an ice-cold beer to wash away the terrors of the night.

His mouth watering at the thought, he raised himself slowly up off the bed and swung his feet onto the floor. He yelped, hopping from one foot to the other as the hot floorboards burned the soles of his bare feet. No wonder he was having bad dreams in this heat. 'It's enough to create havoc with a man's inner self,' he grinned to himself.

As he took a tentative step away from the bed he was aware of a blast of hot air from behind him. Thinking that the hot Savannah wind must be blowing in through the open window, Jesse Gaunt turned and stopped dead in his tracks.

His scream was silent, trapped in his throat. As his eyes widened in total shock, and a chasm of flame opened under his feet, Jesse saw in front of him the apparition that strikes terror into the heart of every good man on God's earth.

He sank to his knees as his legs gave way beneath him, and the dreadful realisation flooded through his brain; the heart-stopping knowledge that his recurring nightmare was the reality, not the dream.

As he watched transfixed, engulfed by the flames licking around him, he saw unspeakable evil reach out to touch him. In front of his unbelieving eyes, the Devil Incarnate reared up on its hind legs, forked tail and cloven hooves slashing through the fetid, fiery air.

As his nightmare reached down to enfold him in its ghastly embrace, Jesse was filled with the terrifying and certain knowledge that he was in the presence of total, unremitting evil. There was no escape from the flames; the fire was all around him, consuming him, devouring him.

Now he knew, finally and irrevocably, the real truth. He had been guilty all along. And this – this was his punishment. The real nightmare was only just beginning.

Great tongues of flame erupted from Satan's dreadful mouth as he glared mercilessly down on the newcomer and intoned in a voice that shook the Underworld:

'Welcome, Jesse Gaunt! We have been waiting for you. Welcome... TO HELL!'

JUST ONE OF THOSE DAYS

Well, I suppose I should have known when the alarm went off and I reached out to turn it off and knocked the glass of water flying. The cat was just walking past at the time; it jumped vertically into the air as the water doused it and landed, claws out, on my naked chest.

By the time the pandemonium subsided and I had stopped screaming, I was late for the train. Plasters on my chest, and reeking of TCP, I raced out of the door, colliding with the milkman and knocking two pints of milk out of his hand. Leaving him fuming in a pool of milk and broken glass, I yelled my apologies over my shoulder as I ran.

At the station the train was just pulling out, an old-fashioned one with doors you can still yank open at a run. Unfortunately, as the train was going faster than I was, I landed face down on the platform, obscenities flying over my head from the fat man sitting in the compartment next to the carriage door I had just opened and which he had slammed shut again.

I got up unsteadily, brushed off any loose dirt, and used a tissue to staunch the bleeding from my cut hands. My knees were very bruised and my nose had ballooned to twice its normal size from its impact with the platform. I endeavoured to saunter nonchalantly back to the Gents' cloakroom, ignoring the titters from the other passengers on the platform, only to find it locked.

It was going to be one of those days, I could tell. The pong of TCP continued to hang around me, but there was nothing I could do to dispel it. You know how it clings; everyone recognises TCP, don't they?

Now what was I to do? No way of cleaning myself up, so what was the plan of action? A later train to the office, or go home and call in sick? Executive decision time.

50/50... and I got it wrong!

I lingered painfully in the warm buffet until the next train pulled in. Without checking the board I gratefully stepped up into the nearest carriage, settled back still wiping my wounds, and waited to be deposited at Waterloo. Well, you know how it is; that creeping realisation that you are not, actually, going in the direction you should be. In fact, you have no idea just where you *are* going. All I knew, as that awful knot-in-the-stomach feeling began, was that I was NOT going to Waterloo.

I appeared to have boarded a train that stopped at no stations, was sparsely populated, and meandered excruciatingly slowly through countryside I could not recognise. Luckily, I had brought my mobile phone with me, but I should have known before I looked. Continuing the day's 100% record, the battery was dead, the phone useless.

My poor nose was throbbing by now, and as I had forgotten my comb, my hair was standing completely on end. I knew from the mirror over the seat, when I sneaked a peek at myself, that I looked like a patient on day release from the local psychiatric unit.

However, the aroma of TCP still strong in my nostrils, I drew myself up to my full height and approached the only other occupant of this particular carriage, in order to ascertain exactly where I was actually going. I had not reckoned on the effect my appearance and emanating odour would have on him.

As he let out a piercing scream and jumped up onto the seat, cowering in terror against the window, I stepped back in alarm and fell over his briefcase on the floor. My head made contact with the door and I saw stars. Not being at all astrologically minded, I did not immediately recognise any of them, but then it WAS broad daylight.

Through streaming eyes, my nose on fire with pain, I watched in horror as my fellow traveller pulled the emergency alarm cord, bringing the train to a screeching halt. As I was already on the floor, I should have been immune from further injury, but unfortunately I was thrown against the iron stanchion under the seat, my poor suffering nose receiving yet another wallop.

My travelling companion remained kneeling on the seat, eyes bulging in terror, and hanging onto the rack above him for dear life. The carriage door was flung open and two burly railway security guards jumped in, demanding to know who had pulled the cord, and why. After much questioning and garbled answers from myself, it was obvious to all of them that I was, indeed, an escaped lunatic.

Understandably in the circumstances, I think, I was taken off the train to the local police station for another bout of interrogation about my strange appearance, my incoherence, and general dazed behaviour. And, of course, the lingering smell of TCP that followed me wherever I went.

Having finally persuaded the local police officers that I was neither drunk nor drugged, and certainly not dangerous, I was accorded the delight of a cup of tea before being escorted back to the railway station. No further action would be taken, I was assured, but it would appear that I had completely unnerved the other gentleman in the carriage, who had needed sedation from the local doctor.

Gentlemen that they were, despite their titters, the kindly constabulary had provided me with some ice cubes to append to my, by now, enlarged and glowing proboscis. The relief was immediate, I must say, but temporary. I felt more like Rudolph the Red-nosed Reindeer than an upstanding member of the Stock Exchange.

I took my leave, offering profuse thanks to the blue-coated members of the nation's law enforcers, but I confess to being a trifle disconcerted as I left the premises to gales of muffled laughter from the assembled throng waving me goodbye.

Anybody would think they had never come across a gentleman in distress before, such hilarity and jocularity issued forth from behind the closing doors of the police station. I threw back my shoulders and, head held high, marched steadfastly away from the scene, my poor nose shining like a beacon through the gloom of the winter's day.

Thoroughly dejected by now, I decided this time to give it up as a bad job. I would return home and take the rest of the day off. Crossing the bridge at the station to the opposite platform, I waited for a train to take me back to my home town. Well, either I was a tad tired, disorientated, or just generally concussed, but the train I should have boarded was, in fact, the one AFTER the train into which I actually hauled myself.

Grateful for the warmth of the carriage, and resigned to losing a day's work at the office, I dozed fitfully as we thundered on southwards through the English countryside. Inevitable though it was following my adventures thus far, I was more than a little mortified to awake as the train pulled into Portsmouth Harbour, a mere 75 miles away from where I actually wanted to be!

Unable to believe my extraordinary run of bad luck, I tottered out of the station into the nearest café and rang the office. My tale of woe occasioned total disbelief that I could make such a hash of a short journey into the

City, confidently getting onto the wrong train not once but twice. The hysterical laughter at the other end of the phone was decidedly unfeeling in the circumstances, I thought. I slammed down the receiver, and wandered out into the cold once again, endeavouring to maintain the proverbial stiff upper lip. Let me tell you, it's not easy with a sore conk!

At least I appeared to be providing a number of people with fun and jollity at my own expense, judging by the amount of laughter I was leaving in my wake.

Thoroughly despondent, and with my nose lighting my way, I decided to make the best of a bad job and spend some time exploring this famous town, which I had not visited before.

I walked the streets towards HMS Victory, intending to enjoy this proud monument to British naval history. Unfortunately, my luck continued as it had begun. As I approached the magnificent vessel, my foot caught in a thick mooring rope snaking across the quay. I tripped and fell headlong, bouncing across the slippery cobblestones and heading unerringly towards the edge of the dock, and on down into the freezing murky waters of Portsmouth Harbour.

I do remember wondering vaguely what the hell my Guardian Angel was doing that morning. Feet up with a heavenly pint of lager and an ethereal fag, no doubt, watching celestial football on Sky T.V. But, fairly obviously, not keeping any kind of a weather eye on me!

It would actually have been all right, despite the temperature of the water and my limited swimming ability – no, it *would* actually have been all right if, as I struggled desperately towards the surface, I hadn't come up underneath the Isle of Wight ferry as she navigated the waters to her berth. Now that, you must admit, was a real stroke of bad luck.

My head made contact fairly heavily with her bottom, knocking me out completely. Probably, in the circumstances and with hindsight, it was no bad thing.

Apparently I had been seen diving into the Solent by a number of seafaring chaps, so I was unceremoniously hauled out toot sweet by a couple of naval divers who were checking for barnacles under the Victory. Yet more laughter followed my rescue, it would seem, but luckily I have no recollection of this.

I was informed later that my dive had only been awarded 5 marks out of 10 – a trifle mean, bearing in mind my total lack of experience, don't you think?

My first memory is that of waking up in a white room in a bed with white sheets, wearing a white paper nightie and no underwear. Quite obviously, I thought I was dead – a fairly logical conclusion after the day's events, I think you'll agree. But no: it was the local hospital, where I had apparently had my stomach pumped, and my bottom had been used as a pincushion for multiple antibiotic injections.

As I came to, I found I was now receiving attention from, or being assaulted by, depending on your viewpoint, an elderly doctor whose accent was thick Liverpudlian, and who seemed to find the whole business hysterically funny. Everybody else seemed to find my catalogue of disasters highly amusing, too.

Naturally enough, I did not.

Nursing the mother and father of all headaches, at the earliest available moment I reclaimed my soaking clothes and left hurriedly, depositing puddles all the way down the corridor. Dressed in the paper gown, disintegrating minute by minute as my sodden jacket soaked through the flimsy material, I fear I looked a sad and sorry sight. Charlie Chaplin couldn't have done better.

But by now I was far too embarrassed to care. I just

wanted to get home. Unfortunately, of course, my wallet was now a few fathoms deep in Portsmouth Harbour, and I had no money or credit cards to my name.

Shivering in my wet clothes, and looking like a refugee from a Third World country, all I could do was throw myself on the mercy of the local Salvation Army. They fed me, dried my clothes and gave me a bed for the night. 'So there are still Good Samaritans in this world,' I thought as I laid my head onto the hardest pillow in the world, and attempted to sleep through the worst night of my life. I still had my pride though - at least, I *thought* I did.

I shall gloss over my return home. Yes, I *did* have to get a taxi. Yes, he *did* get lost. Yes, it *did* end up costing me over £100. Yes, I *had* lost my door key when I took my unplanned dip in the harbour. Yes, the taxi driver *did* insist I broke a window to get in and find the money to pay him. Yes, the alarm *did* go off. Yes, the police *did* arrive, and YES! I *did* have to accompany them to the local police station as I had no identification on me.

Well, what did you expect? A happy ending?

I am now recovering from my adventures, my wounds are healing and I shall be back at work tomorrow, with a bit of luck. I believe it's time I had some good luck for a change, don't you?

Ah, there's the front door bell; probably some kind neighbour calling in to see how I'm getting on.

'Just a moment, be right there! Move out of the way, bloody cat. You started all this, you damned moggy. Let me get to the door. Wouldn't want to fall over you, would I?

MOVE! No, not that way, damn you, you could trip me up and I'd fall right down the stairs. Get out of my way – NO, MIND OUT! Stupid animal, are you deliberately trying to – OH NOOOoooooooooooooooo...'

71

SECOND THOUGHTS

My first thought had been the easy one. It was quite simple really – I was not prepared to share the takings this time. After all the other burglaries we had split the profits 50/50, but not this one. Having made my decision, I was determined to stick to it. After all, I was doing virtually all of the planning these days – all my mate had to do was turn up and follow my instructions. Easy for him. Too bloody easy.

After our first faltering steps into the world of housebreaking, we had evolved smoothly into the perfect team. We had planned the robberies together at first, down to the smallest detail, and carried them out to perfection. The police remained totally baffled, and we continued on our merry way from house to house, secure in the knowledge that we were invincible.

Batman and Robin; Laurel and Hardy; Holmes and Watson – they had nothing on us. We were the Super Duo of the thieving hierarchy, burglars without equal. More like Tom and Jerry, some had said, but little did *they* know.

Not even the most hi-tech alarm system could faze us. These days, with easy access to the Internet, there are few secrets left if you know where to look. Every alarm set-up has its Achilles heel, and we were meticulous in searching for those heels. Hours spent in front of the computer yielded extremely satisfactory results. Someone, somewhere out in cyber space, knows the workings of every surveillance system on the market, and it was simply a matter of sourcing the appropriate website.

We were not too greedy, though. We could have accessed sites showing how to make bombs, where to buy illegal weaponry, and other nasties, but that was not our style. All we needed to know was how to disarm the burglar alarms installed in our chosen targets. Nowhere too fancy, mind, nothing too big. 'Easy Profits' were our watchwords.

In like Stealth bombers, unseen and unheard, then away on our toes into the night. Not a single clue left at the crime scene – nothing to get us on 'Crimewatch' even.

Everything went like clockwork, every single time. Sounds bigheaded, I know, but it's the truth. We chose the houses, we knew when the occupants were away, and we had prior knowledge of the alarms. No problem. We researched every job until we had everything perfectly planned, with no room for error.

We were superb craftsmen too, though I say it who shouldn't. We left no trace of our visits, except, of course, the gaps left by the chosen items which we so carefully removed. There was little for us to worry about. In fact, absolutely nothing, except how much money we had netted on each job, and how to spend it!

The Super Duo were so good, in fact, that it was sometimes days before the house-owner realised we'd been there. This, of course, did not help the police in their enquiries! We scanned the newspaper reports avidly, and watched every T.V. bulletin.

In our own little way, we became quite famous. Serial burglars – that was us. Police forces all over the country were left clueless as we chose our targets seemingly at random. Never the same county twice in succession, our hit-and-run tactics crisscrossed the U.K. from top to bottom, and side to side.

Nobody ever saw us so there could be no description of the dastardly pair. We laughed to think how even the most Holmesian of detectives couldn't get the slightest sniff of who these elusive buggers might be! We'd been mates for so long, back to the little infant school in East Croydon, that we knew each other like brothers. Right couple of Jack-the-Lads; life was for the taking.

At least – I'd thought that up until just recently.

The last country house had yielded such an unexpected haul that even we were amazed. We knew what we *had* been expecting, but in addition to that, the huge old safe had contained a special collection of priceless porcelain from Estonia, en route to a famous London museum for a short-term display. We were like a couple of kids when we found it. Chuffed to bits, we danced around the room as we surveyed the contents of the safe.

It was, quite simply, a fantastic bonus. No word had leaked out about its presence in the country, but we knew at once what it was and how much it was worth to the right buyer. Legal documents in the safe told us all we needed to know about this unexpected windfall.

However, it was at this point that I'd had my first thoughts on the subject of splitting the profits. After all, I was the one who did most of the work. We shared the planning and execution of the burglaries to a point, but it was me who actually disarmed the surveillance systems and organised the whole operation, and it was me who disposed of our ill-gotten gains afterwards.

To my way of thinking, I should therefore receive a higher percentage of the rewards. I had brought the subject up once before, but as I had been threatened with grievous bodily harm, and I am an avowed coward in that direction, I had not pursued the thought except when alone.

I was beginning to see a different side of the bloke I'd known since we were kids. The more successful we became, the worse he got. Temperamental, excitable, irrational at times, he was doing less of the work but still taking his 50% cut. Never giving me the credit I was due, he continued to line his pockets at my expense. And he'd treated himself to a personal arsenal of knives and handguns. Obviously fancied himself as a Capone-style gangster, but it was a major worry for me with his mood swings.

His violent temper tantrums, coupled with the weapons he now possessed, had allowed him to sit on his backside while I planned the next jobs, but in fairness, there was no doubt we were a superb team when the time came. Up until now, apart from the one and only time I'd mentioned the money and come face-to-face with a very sharp knife blade a tad close to my eyeball for my liking, I had let things ride.

This time it was different. The unexpected haul was utterly priceless. These long-lost items could only be sold to underworld buyers, who would keep them in their customised vaults. I would need to find the right source, and it would take time.

In addition, the porcelain would be well-known in the antiques world, so it would need very careful planning to dispose of it safely. Meanwhile, we had to find somewhere special to keep the stuff. Again, that would be my task, as always.

I had already purchased a secure lock-up warehouse on the derelict outskirts of the nearest large town, barred and bolted against the world. Standing away from houses and shops on a patch of wasteland at the edge of a filthy canal, it was the perfect place to hide stolen goods. No windows for prying eyes to see in, thick concrete walls – whoever had built it must have been expecting World War Three to break out at any minute. Its huge rolling steel door was custom-built, and would take a tank to break through it. Across the door itself were thick steel bars which bolted into place to form an impregnable fortress.

The tattooed thug I had bought it from, paying cash, of

course, had been extremely tightlipped about what its original purpose had been, but I was just grateful to find such a secure building for our ill-gotten gains. My imagination ran riot as to the previous owners, from gangland bosses to drug smugglers, but I was not about to ask too many questions. I'd heard about it on the grapevine, and 'mum's the word' when it comes to dodgy dealings. Besides, I value my health too much to get on the wrong side of shady characters like that gorilla.

The stolen goods were, as always, carefully packed into large crates in the van, and transferred to the warehouse in the dead of night from their temporary resting-place in our flat. Our old white Transit van was indistinguishable from thousands just like it, but they do not have the reinforced floor and extra storage space we had built into our specially-converted little number. Nor, presumably, false number plates like ours.

From the 'bunker', as we called the warehouse, the items were taken individually to my expert sources and disposed of quickly and efficiently, for cash. The multitude of huts and outbuildings, and umpteen small boats moored in the vicinity, were perfect cover for our nocturnal comings and goings. A busy little canal-side neighbourhood with a lot going on, nobody took the slightest notice of us, even though they must have been a bit curious about what we did in there.

Even more important to me, this time the financial rewards from the antique haul would be enormous. It was a magnificent coup. My friendly dealers, with their worldwide contacts, would find the best homes for these priceless treasures, and the very, very best prices.

The knowledge that the world's detective networks would be hot on our trail in a very short space of time simply added to the excitement. As usual, they would find nothing to associate us with the crime. Neither of us had a record, and we were not on any police computer. Running around in circles, they would, as always, prove hopelessly inadequate to deal with two such slick operatives.

Adrenalin was running at an all-time high. We were drunk as skunks within a very short time as we celebrated our luck, but the inevitable confrontation with my partner-in-crime was only postponed. I began my onslaught with the confidence that only drink can produce, and homed in on him before it all wore off.

Now began the interminable arguments. I was adamant that the amount of work I had already done, and would yet have to do with this particular consignment, should afford me the major part of the income received. He fought every move I made, once again threatening me with physical violence. Only the thought that I would never find another team-mate like him and, of course, the pain he just might subject me to, stopped me from further verbal battle.

It was, however, after this confrontation that I had my second thoughts about things.

Push came to shove when, after weeks of hard work to ensure I'd found the right person for the job, the fence I was going to use for the antique porcelain, an old mate of mine, found us a single buyer in Argentina. This buyer wanted the entire consignment for himself, and was willing to pay handsomely for it. A very rich villain, he had constructed underground vaults on his estate in the hills above Buenos Aires which housed some of the world's most famous missing works of art. The beautiful china collection would be a major addition to his archives.

Who was I to turn down a fortune? I could retire; live the life of Reilly anywhere I chose. All I had to do was deliver the goods into the dealer's hands, pick up the money and leg it before my partner got wind of the deal.

Simple enough, you'd have thought.

Unfortunately I had miscalculated slightly. Well, more than slightly, actually. I should have had enough sense to know that the devious bugger would have got himself a set of duplicate keys to the bunker. It turned out that he had very carefully removed the originals from my key-ring one night while I was asleep. He took great pleasure in swinging said keys under my nose when I brought up the subject of the porcelain, the night after I had decided to do a runner.

Obviously, the knowledge that he had access to the treasure, and would undoubtedly beat me to a pulp if I tried anything underhand, gave me pause for thought. But not for long. Things would have to be brought forward; it was as simple as that. Transfer of the goods to the dealer must be completed earlier than anticipated, and without 'Mack the Knife' smelling a rat.

I was sure I could do it; after all, my escape route was by now planned in meticulous detail, and I was totally confident in my ability to cut and run. I reckoned I could get away with it, with just a little bit of good luck.

I contacted the dealer on the quiet, and arranged to meet him at the deserted warehouse that same night. He was to bring a van and the cash – simple. He argued vociferously at first, but finally, after much persuasion on my part agreed, albeit reluctantly. I spun him a yarn – I'm good at that – and the new deal was closed.

I arrived at the appointed time, sure that I was on my way to a fortune, only to find my bloody partner standing grinning inside the closed warehouse, waiting for me with a knife in his hand. My face must have been a picture as the massive door swung up and I saw him standing there, like a malevolent spider awaiting his prey. Been a bit too cocky, hadn't I?

How he had found out, God only knew. But he had, and he was in no mood to be placated. He was there for the handover of the porcelain and the money. 50/50, as always, he leered, knife held threateningly close to my throat. I deemed it sensible to agree at that particular moment, but we were both to be thwarted.

My mobile rang as we stood silently facing each other across the concrete room, my brain working like mad on a cover-up story. It was the dealer; he could not get there that night as the money would take another twenty-four hours to come through from the Argentinian's Swiss bank account.

There was nothing for it but to lock and bolt the heavy bunker door and return home, my partner leaving me in no doubt as to what would happen to me should I ever again attempt to cheat him out of his money. There was no doubt he meant what he said. Stupid I may be, but I do not have a death wish.

My second thoughts about him were reinforced by this threat of violence to my person. Somehow, I would see the deal through at the warehouse, and my devious mind now conceived a plan to lock my highly-dangerous accomplice in the soundproof building, and leave him there until nature took its course. I had never contemplated murder before, but it seemed the only way in which I could reap the rewards of my hard work and dispense with his services at the same time.

It was painfully obvious that my own life was now in jeopardy, and neither of us would be able to trust the other in future. I was determined to get it right this time, and escape unscathed with the cash to a bright new future on the other side of the world.

I began to work on the plan in detail. I only had 24 hours to sort it out. How to deliver the porcelain, get rid of the dealer, deal with my partner, grab all the cash and scarper. It had to be perfect planning, split second timing – my forte.

I could do it, of that I was certain. Yes, I know, I

thought that the first time too. Right smart-arse, me, eh! But this time I would be ready. The stakes were too high – I had to get him off my back once and for all.

It was, as you can imagine, in a state of extreme tension that I arrived at the garage the next night, only to find him yet again ahead of me, as expected. His knife was well in evidence, menacingly held at the ready. I knew I had to get this right; my life depended on it.

Only the arrival of the van to collect the goods prevented another altercation. I've never been so relieved to see anybody as I was that night.

As quickly and silently as possible, we loaded the priceless cargo onto the dealer's van, keeping the back open until the briefcase full of crisp, new £50 notes had been handed over and the amount checked. Finally, closing the van doors and securely locking the priceless cargo inside, my contact and his driver shook hands with us both, and drove swiftly off into the night.

Now it was time to put my plan into action. My second thoughts were about to take shape. Returning inside the empty bunker, my mind was in turmoil as I tried to appear cool, calm and collected. As my partner and I stood toe-to-toe in the now empty warehouse, the impregnable doors shut tight against the outside world, he demanded half the money from the case.

I was, of course, expecting that, but it was a real struggle to keep my hammering heart inside my chest!

Waving the knife in my face, he snatched the briefcase from my hand and laid it carefully on the floor of the garage, watching me all the time with a glare that would turn the milk sour. He had brought a black canvas bag with him, ready to pile the cash into, and I let him put it on the floor next to the case.

As he greedily bent down to count out his share of the proceeds, I slipped my hand into my jacket pocket and slid my fingers into the heavy brass knuckle-duster I had put there for the occasion. The knife was still in his hand, and I had to be extremely fast on my feet. The second he took his eyes off me to check the money, I had to move. I was ready, sinews straining, like a tiger waiting to pounce.

Now, this is where it all began to go horribly wrong. What I had not taken into account at all was that I might not be alone in having second thoughts. Stupid, perhaps, but I had been too busy working out my plan of action to think about a double-cross.

Well, let's face it. Matey-boy had terrified me with his threats, he knew, and presumably he would expect me to be cowed into submission and therefore, totally without backbone. He would expect me to cave in, being the coward that I was, and would, of course, have no suspicions at all that I might be planning anything underhand for a second time. Right? WRONG!

Before I knew what was happening he stood up quickly from his kneeling position beside the briefcase, catching me full pelt under the chin with his head and knocking me off my feet, the heavy knuckle-duster flying out of my hand and across the garage.

Yes, yes... I know what you're thinking, I should have seen it coming. It's always so bloody easy with hindsight, isn't it? But I didn't, O.K.? I admit it. I was stupid, careless, over-confident and cocky. Too busy with my own treacherous thoughts to give him any credence for forward planning. That had always been *my* job; he'd just never had to think for himself. I had always done it for both of us.

But tonight he came of age in that department, and it was me who lost out. The shock of it all caught me completely off guard, and he moved so fast and so hard I didn't stand a chance.

I blacked out as the full force of his head hit me under

the chin, and my knees buckled. I came to slowly, lying on the cold concrete floor, my head spinning. I felt sick, my mouth and nose bleeding from the force of the impact.

But the one thing of which I was totally aware through the nausea and the pain was the sound of the big brass key turning in the padlock, and the thick metal barriers being swung down across the massive steel doors... on the outside.

As the awful realisation dawned slowly on my jangling brain cells, I knew that I had been stitched-up, completely and utterly. He had beaten me to it; outwitted me; taken me totally by surprise. I had not even given this twist a single thought as I made my plans. Served me right, really – I usually had every angle sussed, every eventuality worked out. But he had been ahead of me all the way as I stood over him, getting the knuckle-duster ready.

He had been quicker than me. Smarter than me. I had been ready to move, but he was more than ready. Seizing the moment, he had acted before I could, and now, instead of me leaving him to meet his Maker in this silent, soundproof, concrete cell – I was the one locked in, never to get out.

This I knew, without a shadow of doubt, for remember, this had been my plan too. I knew that no amount of yelling, banging on the door, screaming or any other noise would penetrate through to the outside world.

As well as the briefcase and all the money, the bastard had even taken my mobile phone as I lay stunned on the floor. Not an ounce of pity had he shown, but then, to be fair, neither would I have done, had my own plan succeeded. He had simply turned the tables on me. I had been outwitted and I totally acknowledged that fact.

Perhaps he might send someone back to let me out? No, you're right – not a chance.

I had to smile... there was nothing else I could do.

Ironic, isn't it? My second thoughts would now become my epitaph. Every future thought would revolve around my slow, but totally inevitable, demise here in this windowless prison. Panic set in as I began to take stock of the horror I was to face, a horror I had planned for someone else. His living death was now to be my own.

I leave the reader this account of my last days as a highly successful thief, but an incredibly stupid man. It is written, as you see, in my diary while my mind can recall the events. While I am still capable of any kind of coherent thought.

First, second and now – final thoughts.

I fear I must finish here, as my concentration lapses. Jack-the-Lad is no more. Hunger and thirst have done their work. I have become too weak to write.

I have a new companion now; I can feel its brooding presence all around. Soon it will engulf me, overpower me in my solitude as my mind and body submit to its will. My erstwhile sense of humour seems to have deserted me. I can find nothing to laugh about... nothing at all.

Panic and terror – it brings them to me all the time, my new companion. I whisper its name into the lonely darkness, as the minutes ebb away, as my hold on life becomes ever more fragile. My thoughts are totally dominated now by this nightmare newcomer, this dreaded... insanity.

You see, I know that you are reading this only because, of course, I – am dead.

NOVICE

His pager beeped as he came out of the operating theatre. Mr. Richard Cressall, Consultant Obstetrician, read the message on the tiny yellow screen and, with a shout, turned to race down the hospital corridor. Nurses scattered as he ran towards the double swing doors and out into the bright sunlight. He had been operating all morning – now this!

His new Mercedes sports car shimmered under the sun's rays. Gunmetal grey, sleek and magnificent, it was his dream car – only now he would have to sell it. It was his own fault; he should have thought ahead. He looked at his watch. He had to get across town to the new hospital as quickly as possible, and the traffic was always appalling at this time of day.

Sliding quickly into the pale grey leather driving seat, he backed the car out of his personal parking space and shot forward out of the car park, waving a hand in apology to the ambulance attendants who had to jump quickly out of his path.

He fumed as he sat in the first traffic jam, impatient to get to St. Johns and start work there. It took him twenty minutes to cross the busy town and arrive at the new hospital. 'Bloody traffic!' he muttered as he screeched into a reserved parking space and jumped out of the car at a run. The automatic doors opened to allow him through, and he immediately took the nearest lift to the Maternity Suite on the third floor.

Sister Evans was at the Nurses' station, and greeted the specialist with a cheery 'Morning, Mr. Cressall,' noticing at once how agitated he was.

'Your wife's in the delivery room. Please come through and we'll get you gowned up.' He obediently followed the Sister through to the communicating room, where he donned gown and gloves. Pushing open the next set of double doors, he arrived in the delivery room to find his wife in the last stages of labour and his good friend Dr. Peter Marshall in attendance, along with two nurses.

Richard Cressall was very anxious to help deliver his own child; he had waited nine long months for this day, and he was as excited as a little boy on Christmas Eve.

'Hello darling,' he said to his flushed wife, wiping beads of sweat off her forehead. 'How's it going?'

Kerri Cressall glanced up at him and said through gritted teeth: 'Don't ask – bloody ages – hurts like hell. Where have you *been*?' He flashed a look at Peter Marshall which said; 'What now?' His friend grinned back at him as he said; 'She's doing fine, Richard, fully dilated, getting ready to push the next generation of Cressalls out into the world.'

Richard Cressall, at the top of the tree in the obstetric world, suddenly felt like a complete novice here at his wife's side. He had handled so many children's cases over the years, and delivered numerous babies. Yet here he stood, knees trembling and palms sweating, like a first-year student.

He was appalled at his reaction and struggled to regain his composure, breathing deeply as he stroked Kerri's hand and whispered soothing words to her. Mentally he kept reminding himself that he had delivered dozens of babies over the years. Although this was his wife, he reasoned to himself, it would be no different this time.

But, of course, it was. It was totally different. This time it was *his* baby, their first longed-for child. And he was unbelievably nervous. His hands were shaking, and he had to make a tremendous effort to talk normally, to appear nonchalant as his wife began to pant with her exertions.

'I came as soon as I got your message,' he told Kerri. 'I'm here now, darling, you'll be fine.' He found that he could not talk at all easily, his mouth was so dry, and he had to keep licking his lips. Peter Marshall stood grinning at the perplexed father-to-be, finding the situation extremely amusing.

Richard had been present at many births over the years, but the thought of his own child arriving shortly had obviously knocked him completely out of kilter. He wiped beads of perspiration from his own forehead with the back of his gloved hand, then mopped Kerri's face with a cool flannel.

As Kerri groaned loudly, Dr. Marshall checked her progress once more. Richard stood by her head, stroking her hair and muttering encouragement in her ear. He was feeling light-headed, his wife's pain and discomfort affecting him more than he had expected. Peter Marshall was now examining Kerri again – it was time for her to begin pushing and panting.

She grabbed her husband's arm, her nails digging into his skin. As she alternately pushed then panted, both men urged her on, one at each end of her bed. The baby's head appeared, covered in black hair. Richard grinned in delight as he supported his wife's shoulders so that she could look down on the emerging baby, their first-born. He was elated as his tiny child began its journey into the world.

A few more hard pushes and a slippery little boy shot out into the world to be greeted by loving hands. As Kerri lay back exhausted on the pillow, Richard looked down on his tiny son with a fierce pride, and an immediate bond formed between father and child. Peter Marshall left his nurses to tidy the new mother up while he washed the little boy clean then checked him over and weighed him.

Turning to Richard to congratulate him, Dr. Marshall was amazed to find the consultant in a crumpled heap on the floor. Kerri was staring down at him from her bed in wide-eyed disbelief. Open-mouthed, she looked up at Peter Marshall. 'He's a bloody surgeon, for God's sake! I can't believe it! He'll never live this down. Fancy fainting at the birth of his own son!'

She was right about that. The story of the birth and Richard Cressall's fainting fit spread throughout the medical staff in the town, and he had to face a lot of teasing from colleagues as well as patients. He took it all in good part, and joined in the good-natured laughter against himself.

Kerri, however, was adamant when her next two children were born that Richard should not be in attendance, as he was more trouble than she was.

Mortified, the obstetric genius resigned himself to being present at the birth of other people's children, but not his own. Secretly, it was a great disappointment to him, but he acknowledged that he had made a complete fool of himself, and could possibly do so again.

Over the years the legend grew, as legends always do. His daughter and two sons never let him forget the day he passed out as his first-born child entered the world. It became a family tradition to trot out the story on every possible occasion, much to his embarrassment, but he learned to live with it as time passed by.

Years later, however, he had the last laugh when he brought his own first grandson into the world. His daughter-in-law had gone into early labour in the bathroom of her home, and his son had frantically telephoned him, beside himself with worry. Richard had raced over to the house in time to minister to the young woman, who was in a state of near panic until he arrived to calm things down and add his professionalism to the proceedings.

Helping her through the last stages of labour, Richard delivered his grandson with joy and delight. His strong, capable hands gently brought the precious child into the world as they had delivered so many babies over the years.

Once again, the tumult of emotions he had felt at the birth of his own son all those years ago flooded through him as he tenderly cradled the perfect new family member. He was the first of the new generation of Cressalls, a very important young man.

Then, handing him to his mother, Richard turned his attention to his eldest son, who had fainted dead away at the sight of his child's premature arrival, and lay prone on the floor. Watching in amazement as he placed a cold flannel on the young man's white face, his daughter-in-law cuddled her new son and giggled.

Richard looked up at her with a big grin on his face as his son remained stretched out on the floor, overcome by the emotion of the occasion.

Hugging her baby to her, the new mother looked fondly at the two men and laughed in delight.

'Just wait till I tell Kerri,' she said. 'Talk about like father, like son!' She grinned at Richard as the novice grandfather smiled back, lovingly surveying the all-too-familiar scene.

FULL CIRCLE

I don't remember when I first decided to kill him – the days have become blurred in my mind. I knew that I simply could not go on like this; his drunken rages, daily now; the continual beatings; my living Hell. They all had to be stopped somehow, and there just seemed to be no other solution.

My face is always puffy and swollen these days, the livid cuts and bruises never having time to heal before the next onslaught. My body is black and blue from his punches and kicks, my mind damaged forever by his obscene behaviour.

But it is my heart, above all else, my heart, which suffers the most. Torn apart irreparably, it will never recover from the emotional trauma he has set in motion.

I have not been outside for days, and friends have been told that I have the 'flu, so not to visit in case they catch the bug. I cannot bear the thought of explanations – it would be impossible to lie plausibly.

He had always been such a sweet man until the problems at work started. As the staff numbers were slashed by the new owners after the takeover, and it became a lottery as to who would keep their jobs, he began to drink under the strain of it all. Over the weeks our life together had become intolerable.

He would go straight to the pub from work and stay there until closing time, arriving home totally drunk and incoherent. He lost control of his temper as soon as he staggered through the door, violent and abusive. This was always followed swiftly by a matching loss of control of his bladder, like a child.

My original heartfelt pity had been turned to terror by his inability to curb the violence of his anger, displaying a temper that had not raised its head over the years unless severe frustration or anger prompted an outburst. As quickly as the anger rose, it had always subsided before.

But the man I had known for 25 years had changed beyond recognition. Accepting initially that he had to do something to cope with the worry of losing his job, I knew beyond any doubt that he was now totally out of control.

That we loved each other very dearly, and always had, was not an issue. We were trying to deal with a different set of circumstances here; circumstances which had changed the gentle person I had lived with for so long into a drunken, vicious bully, unable to live with himself or with me.

I bore the brunt of the drinking and the violence. Somehow, by the morning he was sufficiently recovered to go into the office. I did not understand how his body could cope, but cope it did. Mine did not.

I genuinely believe that no-one else in the world had the slightest idea of what was happening to this once gentle, caring man. It was I, and I alone, who bore physical and emotional testimony to the total change in character of the man I loved.

At first he had shown terrible remorse at the sight of the bruising and my swollen face, and the way I flinched every time he came near me. But now even that had stopped. I lived in terror and dread of him coming home at night, knowing that, yet again, he would be unable to stop himself from lashing out, oblivious in his drunken state to what he was doing or saying. He would take his pent-up worries about the future out on me.

There was no escape unless I left him, ran away from the torment. That I knew I could not do. I had nowhere to go, nowhere to hide.

And yet I still loved him... and I hated him.

Tonight, I waited trembling in the kitchen, my face a terrible mess yet again, and my stomach, where he kicked me last night, so painful that I could hardly stand. My hands were sweating, and I felt physically sick as I heard him fumbling with the key in the lock. I stood as far in the corner as I could get, knowing with a terrible certainty that if he attacked me again tonight, I would defend myself with whatever I could find to hand. If, that is, I had any strength left for retaliation.

Maybe he wouldn't hit me... maybe it would be all right. Hope flickered briefly, then was extinguished at once as he staggered through the door.

One glance at him told me it would not be all right.

His face was puce, his once-beautiful blue eyes like ice, and his mouth twisted in rage at the sight of me cowering there. He lurched across to me, fists raised as he screamed his vitriol in my face. I knew then that I had no choice. There would never be an end to this nightmare.

I would carry out the unspoken thought, the unthinkable action.

Terrified, I shrank away from him, but it was hopeless. There was no escape; I was cornered.

His face was so close to mine, the stench of whisky strong in my nostrils. He held my arms so tightly that I cried out, but the vicious mouth kept on, a never-ending outpouring of filth, the man I had loved so dearly calling me every degrading name under the sun. I could neither speak nor move. I seemed to be paralysed by this snarling, spitting entity I no longer recognised.

As the pain in my arm decreased momentarily, I knew he was getting ready to hit me. I felt him raise his fist, and tried to duck, but the blow caught me on my ear and sent me reeling. I fell to the floor, and he kicked me hard in the stomach. I lay there sobbing for breath, every inch of my body aching, my lungs screaming for air.

Sensing him standing over me, staggering to keep his balance, I pulled myself slowly and painfully up against the sink, my hand slipping into the basin. My trembling fingers closed on the kitchen knife I had used earlier to peel the potatoes. I watched as though through a fog as he took another step towards me, raising his arm again to arc down on my face.

As if in a dream, I saw his fist so close to my eyes, and I jabbed hard into his stomach with the knife, feeling it slip into his flesh with surprising ease. As the knife hit home his fist connected with the bridge of my nose with such force that the world went black. The explosion of pain and blood blinded me to what was happening, and I clung onto the sink as I tried to stay upright.

I must not fall again, I knew. The thought pierced through my fuddled brain. I would be lost, unable to bear the pain. He would kick me senseless if I fell – I had to stay on my feet.

When the wave of nausea cleared and the room swam back into focus, I could see him on his knees in front of me. His eyes were wide with shock as he clumsily tried to hold the spreading pool of blood on his shirt. He looked up at me, those beautiful blue eyes now showing pain and... what was that, disbelief? Yes, total disbelief.

With my own blood now running down from my nose into my mouth and onto my clothes from the vicious punch to my head, there came my own shocking loss of control. I stood looking down into the face of the man I had loved for such a very long time, disgust overwhelming me at that moment. As he opened his mouth to speak, I moved behind him and, putting my foot onto his back, kicked out with all my might so that he toppled forward onto the floor, the knife driving deep into his stomach.

Apart from a muffled groan he made no sound. Shaking uncontrollably, I knelt down, wiping blood from my face with the back of my hand. I turned him over onto his back, seeing only the handle of the knife sticking out from his body, and knowing that such a massive loss of blood must bring death very quickly.

His eyes were wide open, staring sightlessly up at me. There was no movement at all. I looked down into his face through a mist of blood and tears. I had no feelings left now – I was numb, utterly exhausted.

I watched those eyes cloud over as his breathing finally stopped, but I felt nothing except relief that the pain and terror was over. I had killed the only person I had ever truly loved, but for now time stood still there in my kitchen.

Through my pain and exhaustion reality came creeping back little by little, as I stood trembling over the body of the man I had only recently grown to hate. The numbness slowly began to recede, and my thoughts became clearer as the fog inside my head lifted like a curtain.

I knew, with sudden clarity, that one day, at some time in the future when I had to account for my actions, I would need help to cope with what I had done. Despite the knowledge and the certainty that I had killed this man in self-defence, before he could kill me, I knew that there would be a day of reckoning for me.

That would be the fateful day when I would have to acknowledge the enormity of my actions; the day when I would finally understand just what I had really done tonight. Through my increasing pain came the realisation that my life would never be the same again. I had stepped over the threshold into a new world, a new future – and I would have to pay a terrible price.

My thoughts tumbled over themselves as they filtered through the unreality surrounding me, the insanity of the situation impinging itself mercilessly on my whirling brain. I stood there, cold with shock at what this would mean for me, the enormity of what had happened here tonight.

I had taken a life, a life once so very precious to me. I would be called to account, to explain such a sudden death; to tell my story. There would doubtless be sympathy and understanding for my plight, but I knew I would pay dearly for my actions. Retribution would be expected and pursued relentlessly. My motive and my mentality questioned ad infinitum.

But that was in the future. For now, as I stared down at the lifeless, blood-soaked body on my kitchen floor, I knew without a shadow of a doubt that I had had no choice. I knew that a monster had taken over the body and mind of my loved one; had taken root within him and changed him beyond recognition.

I knew that death had been the only release for him and for me. There had been no other way to free us from his dreadful metamorphosis.

The blue eyes, once so very bright, remained blank and unseeing as I tearfully stared down into them for the last time.

Slowly, so very slowly, I sank to my knees beside him, and took his once-dear face gently into my hands. Through my tears I spoke quietly and lovingly – a few words for him to take on his journey.

A few last words of love from a mother to her only son.

A MATTER OF GRAVE CONCERN

They gathered together every night under the ancient yew tree in the old graveyard. It was a perfect place to hold their meetings; no-one would disturb them here. Once darkness fell, they knew that only the creatures of the night would be out and about. Bats, owls, mice and rats, together with the occasional fox, were their only visitors.

Tonight was a special occasion. They had a particular topic to discuss. Once they had all arrived and were sitting in a circle on the well-tended grass, the matter of old Mrs. Simpkins was brought into the conversation, and an animated discussion began to find a way in which the old lady could be helped.

It had been noticed by many of the assembled company that the poor old dear was having trouble looking after her husband's grave. She had been a widow for many years and visited the graveyard regularly. Recently, though, it had become more and more obvious that she was having difficulty in clearing the weeds from the small patch of earth as she grew older and more infirm. She had tried to scrub the discoloured white marble clean too, but it was hopeless.

The tiny angel on the headstone had weathered badly over the years, and the old lady's distress at being unable to restore it to its original beauty was heartbreaking. Many times they had seen her leave the cemetery in tears, knowing she was going home to an empty house, and they shared her sorrow at the state of her husband's memorial.

Her arthritic fingers made it so difficult to hold a

scrubbing brush and, hard though she tried, the years had taken their toll on the marble. Nothing could bring it back to its original pristine perfection, and Mrs. Simpkins could not afford to have the stone cleaned professionally.

Several of those attending the meeting had tried quietly in their own way to help her, but she was a fiercely proud old lady. This was her private grieving place, somewhere she could talk to her husband while she tidied his grave and placed fresh flowers on it. It was her wish to look after his resting-place on her own; even friends and neighbours were not allowed to help her. They could visit and put flowers there, but she would not let them weed the tiny flower-bed. That was her duty, she told them firmly, and she must do it for her Albert. They had been a devoted couple, and she missed him very much.

The question was: just how could they help Mrs. Simpkins look after the grave and keep it as immaculate as ever, without upsetting her or seeming to interfere? It was vital that she believed she was in sole charge of this small piece of land here in the cemetery, but it was also obvious to them all that she could no longer cope without some kind of assistance.

All those present had watched at one time or another as the ageing widow had tried to do the weeding, her arthritis causing her such pain that it sometimes made her cry. They had wanted to rush to her aid, but they knew she would become angry at her shortcomings and they would simply make matters worse, despite their good intentions.

She was a kindly old lady, and whenever she had had time in the past, she had also tidied some of the more overgrown graves in the churchyard. Any flowers left over from her husband's grave had been placed on others which seemed neglected. Now it was all she could do to keep his tiny garden tidy and neat, and they knew that this distressed her terribly.

Various ideas were put forward and talked through, but it did not prove easy for them to find a way to help in this matter which would not upset Mrs. Simpkins. They decided to sleep on it and meet again as usual the next night.

Setting aside the problem for the present, they continued with their lively conversation until the younger members decided it was time they went home.

At their next meeting, under a full moon and a clear sky sprinkled with bright stars, one of the older members of the group came up with an idea which he thought might help. It should be possible for them to take it in turns to keep Albert's grave spick and span, he reckoned, so that when Mrs. Simpkins arrived on her daily visits, not much work would be needed and she could simply replace the flowers. A little weeding now and then would probably keep her happy, and she may not notice how little she actually needed to do, if they were clever about it.

They would have to be very careful how much tidying and cleaning they did, but if they did just a little at a time, it should not be too obvious to the old lady.

Pleased with this sensible suggestion, they all nodded in agreement. A rota would be drawn up and each one of them would look after the grave in turn. They would also watch Mrs. Simpkins very carefully to see her reaction to what they were doing.

Satisfied with this solution to the problem, and looking forward to assisting the old lady, the first few helpers were chosen, and at dawn the following morning they began their work.

Mrs. Simpkins puffed her way along the winding path through the graveyard, dreading the thought of getting down on hands and knees to take out the weeds that sprang up constantly, despite all her efforts. She was getting too old for this, she thought to herself, but she would never admit as much to anybody. Albert had been her childhood sweetheart, and they had been married for over fifty years. The least she could do was to keep his resting place neat and tidy until she joined him there.

As she rounded the last corner, she had to sit down on the bench under the old yew tree to catch her breath. She could see the grave from here. 'How funny,' she thought. It looked to her as though the marble headstone was cleaner than usual, and the tiny angel looked more like it used to, white and quite beautiful. It had weathered badly over the years, but today it looked brighter than normal.

She got up and walked slowly over to inspect the old stone. The sun was shining down from a clear blue sky, and she thought perhaps it was simply the bright light glinting off the marble. Her old eyes must be playing tricks, she thought. But it certainly did look as though a lot of the dirt had gone. She glanced around, but there was no-one in the churchyard she could ask about it.

There were only a couple of weeds, too. Thank goodness for that: not too much kneeling today. She was very grateful; it was becoming so difficult for her to tend the grave these days, but it would not take her long to clear the tiny patch this afternoon. Her aches and pains forgotten, she set to work with a happy heart.

From their hiding places the conspirators watched with pleasure as the old lady quickly picked out the few weeds they had left for her, and saw the happiness on her face as she stood with head bowed in prayer. They had not cleaned the marble too much, just enough to brighten it up a little. It did look much better, and she was obviously pleased by its appearance. She had seemed puzzled at first, but they were delighted to see that, after weeding the little garden, she was no longer concerned about the subtle changes to the headstone.

Every day after that, when Mrs. Simpkins arrived to visit Albert, there were only a few weeds to worry about, and her fresh flowers took pride of place. Her kindly old face lit up to see how good the grave was looking these days, and how little work she had to do. It made life so much easier for her, and her concern had disappeared as the little plot remained immaculate for the world to see.

The nightly meetings took on a special air of happiness, everyone so pleased to help the old lady without her knowing. It was lovely to see the change in her, her joy at the beauty of the little marble angel.

Then one night, something rather wonderful happened. As they all took their places amongst the gravestones, a new visitor joined them. They turned to see old Albert Simpkins making his way slowly towards them, stepping carefully and respectfully round the memorials. They all got up to welcome him, and bring him into the friendly gathering.

At first he was a little nervous, but they made him comfortable and settled him down on the grass. It was his first time, but his new friends took him under their wings and made him feel very happy, part of the family.

He thanked them for what they were doing for his wife. He had watched it all, and his old eyes filled with tears of gratitude. They took it in turns to hug him, and made him promise to join them every night from now on. He was with friends, they told him, surrounded by love and peace.

Knowing that it would not be long before his beloved wife would be here with them too, Albert and the other ghosts of the graveyard settled down for their nightly get-together. Unseen and unheard, the benevolent spirits enjoyed the closeness and friendship they had formed over the years, their numbers growing as more and more crossed over to that other world.

Albert returned later to his perfect little garden, so lovingly tended by his dear wife. Everyone else had gone home too. He looked at the flowers so fresh and lovely, and thought of his beloved Ada, his dear girl.

'Soon, my love, soon,' he whispered. And he gently reached out his hand to touch the beautiful marble headstone with its tiny guardian angel, tenderly tracing her name with his finger, underneath his own.

A FAIRY TALE

The Fairy sat up on the Christmas tree,
Looking so pale and forlorn.
It's orl right for them, she was thinking.
They stick me up 'ere then they're gorn!

The family's cleared orf an' gorn shoppin',
The dog's cocked 'is leg on me tree.
A Fairy 'as feelings, so stoppin'
Up 'ere could be dodgy for me!

They stuck me right up on the top 'ere,
Me vertigo's rampant as 'ell.
What I need is a bottle of brandy.
If I'm drunk I'd not care if I fell.

I could do with a fag, but I can't reach
That packet way down on the floor.
What a way to be'ave to a Fairy!
Bloody Christmas, and need I say more?

The cats are both knockin' me bells orf.
I'm fed up and lonely to boot.
It's not a nice way to spend Christmas,
But they obviously don't give a hoot.

They think I look cute and so pretty,
Guess I do when the candlelight flickers.
But they rammed me down 'ard
When I let down me guard,
There's a bloody great branch up me knickers!

DANCING QUEEN

Tuesday night at the Palais – 70's Night. They were all there, as usual, dressed up to the Nines in the cosmopolitan clothes from that flamboyant era. Anything goes on 70's Night, and the Palais was alive with the fashions and hairstyles from the disco years. Gaudy make-up, platform shoes, miniskirts, maxi dresses, flared trousers, tight satin shirts and lots of Afro wigs – everyone had pulled out all the stops to Do the Time Warp again.

The loud music blared unceasingly from the banks of amplifiers, and the dancers gyrated blissfully under the strobe lights. All shapes, sizes and ages, their common love of disco music brought them all here together. This was *their* night, and they came from miles around to share in the weekly party.

A panacea for everyday worries and problems, and an opportunity to forget the cares of the world – that was 70's Night at the Palais.

Taking pride of place, in her usual fashion, Doreen strutted her stuff to the delight of the crowds, the spotlight picking her out from time to time as she performed her John Travolta dance steps under the glittering silver ball suspended from the ceiling. The lights bounced off the mirrored globe as it slowly revolved, showering beams of iridescent silver onto the dancers pressed together out on the floor.

Dressed in a tight red leather mini skirt, saucy black blouse, and with her long blonde hair swinging sensuously as she danced to the music, Doreen drew admiring glances from the girls and lecherous leers from the men.

She was a regular on Tuesday nights, and, dressed to kill, always left a lasting impression as she sashayed the night away. A Disco Queen par excellence.

She was something of an enigma, was Doreen. Nobody seemed to know much about her, and she always managed to disappear after the evening's energetic dancing in a Cinderella-like fashion, vanishing into the night without anyone seeing her go. She was a friendly soul, very attractive with her pretty hair and slim figure. She loved to swap gossip with the locals, and was the best dancer the Palais had seen in a very long time.

Even so, apart from her name and her fantastic disco dancing, little else was known about her. Shy and retiring she definitely was not, but she always arrived alone and left alone.

Appearing every Tuesday as the doors opened at 7 o'clock, she disco-ed the night away until the last notes faded out on the stroke of midnight. Her outfits were the envy of the ladies, and she invariably wore out more partners in one evening than seemed possible. Accepting the odd drink from male admirers, and revelling in her celebrity status, she sparkled and twinkled the 70's Nights away, only to disappear at the end of the evening, not to be seen again until the following Tuesday.

All attempts at dating were rebuffed, gently but firmly, and after many weeks of attempting to glean her phone number, address or any other personal information, Doreen remained a closed book to the many hopeful men who crossed her perfumed path on the dance floor.

Tall and slim, her lovely hair always immaculately groomed, the Disco Queen wore her clothes with a flourish. One week she would choose the maxi look, the next it would be a mini skirt. Impeccably made up, and beautifully turned out, it was impossible to guess her age.

There were some who remarked cattily that, 'She's a bloody sight older than she looks,' but her incredible dancing skills turned heads week after week. For hours she would whirl and twist, totally lost in the music, while the resident DJ played so many well-remembered songs from the long-ago era. She would wave back at him with a dazzling smile when he called her name out over the microphone.

She was undoubtedly the star of Tuesday evenings at the Palais. Everyone knew her, and she was always in the spotlight as she boogied her way through the hours to midnight. Never wanting for partners, she dispatched man after man to the bar as they failed to keep up the pace. Gasping for breath and demanding a pint, one by one they fell by the wayside as she continued her dancing with only the occasional break for a trip to the powder room.

Her Cinderella disappearing act simply added to the mystery of the lovely lady, but, totally unconcerned by any gossip she might be generating, Doreen continued her love affair with the music of the 70's at the Palais. She was unstoppable as she twirled and whirled under the circling silver ball. Always in the middle of the dance floor, never at the edge, Doreen was in her own special world as the music played on. Giving it her all, and dominating the scene, she had long since become a local legend.

Her shining mane of blonde hair swung sensuously as she danced and danced and danced. 'A beautiful mover,' was a comment often heard from the admiring watchers. There were a number of saucy comments too, and Doreen's lips twitched with delight whilst she pretended not to hear them.

She adored all the attention, especially from the men. Dressed like a vamp tonight, she smirked to herself as she gave them a display to knock their socks off and get the blood pounding in their veins. Bumping and grinding to the beat, she could almost feel their hormones working overtime.

'Oh you wicked woman!' she thought with a grin as she moved her hips provocatively in time to the music. She was well aware of her sensuality and the effect it had on the male population at the Palais, and she revelled in the knowledge that she was wreaking havoc with her erotic dancing. Always ready with a quip and a gentle riposte to any overt sexual advance, she nevertheless enjoyed flaunting herself in front of her adoring audience.

In the Ladies' cloakroom, she would natter with whoever else was in there while they powdered their noses, and, apart from the ever-present posse of resident bitches, she was well-liked by both male and female supporters of the evening. Tonight, as ever, she was the Belle of the Ball, the Palais' very own Dancing Queen.

Adjusting her tiny skirt and checking that her blouse was showing the maximum amount of cleavage, Doreen re-applied her lipstick and blusher. Dancing was such a pleasure to her, but the perspiration did turn her make-up patchy in places so she did some running repairs with a powder puff, then surveyed herself in the mirror.

'Lovely,' said a voice in her ear, and she turned her disarming smile on the pretty girl standing next to her in the tiny cloakroom. 'You look lovely, Doreen.'

'Thanks dear,' she said sweetly to the youngster, and brushing her long hair back into place, checked her appearance once more in the mirror before opening the door and returning to her place in the centre of the dance floor.

After a few weeks of her stunning displays under the spinning silver ball, she had become a celebrity in her own right. Her love of dancing was obvious to the crowds that packed out the Palais on Tuesday nights, and her sheer joie de vivre created a party atmosphere among her fellow devotees as they bowed to their Leader, Doreen the Magnificent.

As her popularity increased, there were a number of people who tried to find out just where she went when she left, but mostly they respected her wish for privacy away from the Palais. She had perfected the art of slipping away without being noticed. Then up she would pop the following Tuesday, to repeat her magical gyrations for the world to watch in admiration and adulation.

Tonight was no exception. She had, as usual, slipped out of the back exit as the lights dimmed and the music faded. Carefully choosing her moment, she glided quickly through the heavy door and into the waiting minicab before anyone noticed she had left.

Like a Will-o-the-Wisp, one minute she was there, the next she was gone.

Laying her head back on the seat as the driver pulled away from the kerb, she laughed with delight at the pleasure the evening had yet again given her. She adored the Palais, and the music of the 70's had always been her favourite. It was such a wonderful evening; she looked forward to it every week with excited anticipation. Every day at work she thought about the previous Tuesday with utmost pleasure, and worked out what she would wear the next time.

Her whole life revolved around her Tuesday nights. She lived to dance, and the Palais was her stage. Everything else paled into insignificance compared to her weekly dance evenings. Every spare moment was filled with choosing her outfits and deciding how she would wear her hair. She knew the effect that she had on the men, and loved to think that she was such a favourite with the crowds.

Closing her eyes and reliving the night's excitement,

Doreen felt the adrenalin pumping, tired though she was. It always took her a long time to get to sleep after a night's dancing, she was on such a high.

As the driver stopped the minicab outside the address she had given him, Doreen leaned over his seat and paid him the usual amount, plus a large tip. 'Thanks love,' he said with a smile. 'Same time next week?'

She smiled and nodded, sliding gracefully across the back seat and out into the night. 'Goodnight,' she said in her husky voice, 'and thank you so much.'

'Lovely girl,' the taxi driver thought to himself. 'Don't say much, but it's regular money. If she wants to keep 'erself to 'erself, that's O.K. by me.' Grinning lecherously at the sight of Doreen's mini-skirted bottom wiggling its way up the pavement as she tripped along on her stiletto heels, he drove off into the night with his mind full of erotic fantasies about blonde disco dancers.

Turning the key in the front door lock, Doreen slipped quickly inside and shut the door behind her. Kicking off the high-heeled shoes, she leaned back against the wall with a sigh of relief as she massaged one sore foot with the other, smiling again at the memory of the night's success, and her dancing prowess as the Disco Queen.

Switching on the hall light, she stood for a moment checking her appearance in the wall mirror. 'Not bad,' she thought with a grin. 'Not bad at all.' Smoothing her lovely long hair into place, she smiled at her reflection with satisfaction.

As she turned to climb the stairs to her bedroom, a voice from upstairs stopped her in her tracks. Her heart seemed to stop beating as she heard a girl's voice call out, 'Is that you?'

Numb with shock, Doreen held onto the wall for support as beads of sweat broke out on her forehead. Closing her eyes, and feeling faint and dizzy, she whispered, 'No! Oh please God, no.'

The voice came again, getting nearer now. Doreen's daughter Lorna appeared at the top of the stairs, chattering on about getting home early for once; how it was an unusually quiet night on the wards; how she could really use some sleep; hoped it wasn't too much of a shock to find her at home, etc. etc. As she focused through the dim light in the hallway on the exhausted disco dancer leaning against the wall at the bottom of the stairs, Lorna abruptly broke off from her chatter in mid-sentence with a sudden sharp intake of breath.

For what seemed an eternity, parent and child stood motionless, staring at each other. Then the silence was broken by a piercing scream from Lorna, echoing through Doreen's head and shattering her dreams into a million pieces.

Slumped against the wall and gazing up at the screaming girl in utter despair, the erstwhile Dancing Queen began to sob quietly as Lorna grew increasingly hysterical.

There was nothing to be done now, it was too late.

Lorna should not have been at home. She should have been on duty at the hospital, like she was every Tuesday night.

But she was not – she was here. And Doreen's world would never be the same again.

Wiping away the tears with the back of his hand, Lorna's father slowly took off his long blonde wig and haltingly began to climb the stairs towards his screaming daughter.

THE AUTHORESS

'Eve Adams would like to point out that,
despite rumours to the contrary,
this story is not based on herself!'

She sat in front of her word processor, rollers in her dyed blue hair and a cigarette hanging out of the corner of her mouth. Ash dripped steadily down the front of her faded sugar-pink housecoat, adding to the multitude of stains already festering there. It was difficult to tell which was the most bedraggled and tatty, the writer or her housecoat.

Peppered with tiny burn marks from cigarettes spilling regularly from her mouth, the once-pretty robe bore testament to the hygiene standards of its owner. Dirty and grime-laden, it was far too late to respond to a wash; much the same could be said of the lady wearing it. Incineration was the only recourse now for faithful old housecoat. It had done its best over the years, and given sterling service, but resurrection was out of the question – it was beyond help.

A cup of cold coffee stood on her desk with a light film of mould on its surface, leaving yet another brown ring on the wooden worktop. Cake and biscuit crumbs sprinkled the keyboard, jamming the keys as she half-heartedly drummed her fingers on them. Sighing heavily, she inhaled deeply on the drooping cigarette, blowing a thick cloud of smoke out through her nose and obscuring the screen in front of her.

Her fat ginger cat lay sprawled on the threadbare carpet under the workstation while the grubby off-white terrier snuffled through yesterday's pizza box left on the floor to putrefy. Emerging from the cardboard with a bright red nose, it sneezed the rancid tomato topping all over its owner's heavily blue-veined bare feet, but she did not notice.

All around the room remnants of previous takeaways grew mould faster than a penicillin laboratory, and the stench of stale food filled the air. She puffed away at her cigarette, never taking it out of her mouth. A chain-smoker, there were ashtrays piled high with dog-ends littering the small room, adding to the stale aroma permeating the atmosphere. The room was permanently filled with a heavy pall of smoke, and her smoker's cough rattled up from the bottom of her lungs as she dragged deeply on the untipped cigarettes constantly glued to her lower lip.

Today was not a creative one. At times like this she wished she had never taken up writing. Her first book had been a worldwide bestseller and now she had to come up with a sequel. It was too much like hard work – she needed a drink.

Although it was only ten o'clock in the morning, she poured herself a large whisky from one of the many bottles standing on the small round table within easy reach of her desk. The number of dirty glasses already scattered around the room attested to the fact that this was not her first today.

The grubby dog nosed round her ankles, wiping the remaining tomato sauce onto her feet, and she viciously kicked it away. It slunk off into the corner pausing only to glare up at its owner, hatred written clearly on its face. The ugly ginger cat continued to slumber, totally oblivious to the dog's discomfort, and the authoress sat heavily back on the chair in front of her monitor, tipping it over at a dangerous angle with her bulky torso.

Years of neglecting her body had left their mark. Rolls of fat overlapped the seat as she once again assumed the writing position. Sumo wrestling would have been better suited to her than writing, built as she was like a brick outhouse, but it was not a career she had considered to date.

Moodily she glared at the blank screen, trying to dredge up some kind of idea from the dark recesses of her mind. Her nerves were frayed to their ends as she idly contemplated suicide as an alternative to this heinous existence, but she dismissed the thought as soon as it entered her head. It was, however, to be the only thought she could summon up for the time being.

Stubbing out her cigarette and immediately lighting another, she downed the whisky in one gulp, belching loudly as the fiery liquid hit her stomach. The noise reverberated around the small room, echoing back from the smoke-grimed walls, but she ignored it and continued her vigil in front of the empty glowing screen.

Unkempt and untidy, she cared not a hoot how she looked. The word 'slovenly' could have been coined especially for her. She was a mess, the house was a mess, but she didn't give a damn. This was her inner sanctum; intruders were not tolerated here. Struggling to recapture the magic of her first tome she remained oblivious to the outside world.

Dust collected over the furniture, and the post lay unopened in the hall. Nothing mattered except her writing, but the screen remained empty, as did her brain cells. The rollers were slowly unravelling in the dyed blue locks, as she shook her head vigorously in an effort to trigger some appropriate opening words, revealing long black roots much in need of a touch-up.

'Bugger this for a lark!' she muttered. Reaching down over her enormous belly she opened the door to the small fridge under her desk, disturbing the ugly ginger tom as she did so. As the obnoxious animal spat at her, receiving a smack on its snout in return, she took a can of ice-cold beer out of the fridge and proceeded to struggle upright again. Ripping off the ring pull, she gargled the beer down greedily, belching again as it joined the whisky already slopping around inside the cavernous stomach. Her eyes crossed momentarily as the cold beer hit her solar plexus, and she hiccupped twice to restore the status quo.

Staring once again at the screen she sighed loudly, launching ripples of fat down her elephantine body like a big pink jelly wobbling on a plate. The rollers shook with the momentum, dangling precariously at the very ends of her greasy two-toned hair.

The phone rang incessantly out in the hall, but she could not be bothered to get up and answer it. Here in her study she was cocooned in her own little world, a perfect oasis of grimy squalor from which would emanate a world-beating manuscript... eventually.

Unfortunately for the authoress, today was more of a struggle than usual. The words simply would not come, and she had absolutely no idea how she could follow her successful first book. 'Writer's block,' they called it.

'Well, bugger 'em!' she said with her usual delicacy of diction. 'I'm not giving in that easily.'

Lifting one huge cheek off the seat she suddenly broke wind with such force that both the dog and the cat jumped vertically like two mini Harrier jets. A stream of cigarette ash rippled down onto her lap but she took no notice. There was a pile of it now in the folds of her housecoat, ready to be jettisoned onto the obscenely rancid carpet when she finally moved her bulk out of the chair.

The cat dug its claws into her ankle in its fury at being disturbed, and she kicked out at it, sending it snarling and spitting to take cover under the armchair. It hissed its venom at her from the safety of the big chair with its moth-eaten covers.

Draining the contents of the can, she levered herself up into a standing position and wandered over to the window. She could see nothing through the filthy glass. Cleaning windows was not one of her passions, similarly housework in general. She stood smoking by the disgusting net curtain, adding another layer of brown stain to the disintegrating material. It hung in tatters, unwashed since the day it had been put there.

The cat and the dog watched her warily from their positions of safety. They knew better than to disturb her when she was in this kind of mood. For their own sakes it would be better to stay where they were, out of reach. They exchanged knowing glances across the litter-strewn floor and retreated further into their refuges, where she could not touch them. For her to bend so far down was impossible; this they knew from her previous futile attempts, and each smugly curled up into a ball to doze away the morning.

Moving her mountainous body away from the window and wiping her nose on the sleeve of the ragged pink housecoat, she delved into the huge box of chocolates on the table, stuffing three at once into her mouth. Cheeks blown out like a hamster with mumps, she chewed loudly with her mouth open, dribbling chocolate down her chin and once again, onto the grubby robe.

Using her sleeve this time to wipe her chin, adding streaks of chocolate to the patchwork of colours and odours, she lumbered back to her seat in front of the monitor. As she sat down heavily she again broke wind, lifting the back of the housecoat several inches into the air. Neither dog nor cat responded this time, each curled up with their paws over their ears, a self-defence position learned from bitter experience.

Smacking another couple of chocolates noisily around in her mouth, the writer absent-mindedly picked at a festering boil on the first of her many chins, her grubby fingernails finishing off any chance the offending pustule might have had of disappearing quietly. Once again using her sleeve as a blotter, she dabbed at her chins, following up with another quick wipe of her nose, while she was in the vicinity.

Tucking her bare feet, badly in need of a touch of soap and water, back under the desk, she continued to glare at the empty screen. Reaching down for another can of beer from the fridge, she froze mid-way as a thought struck her.

If she stuck to the same subject as before, and simply elaborated and enlarged certain points, she could create another book similar to the first.

The sequel. Part 2. Volume II. More of the same.

The first book had created a sensation. Why not stick with the winning formula?

Relief flooded through her. That was the answer! A second book on the same lines as the first. Why on earth hadn't she thought of it before? Good grief, it was so simple after all.

Hauling herself up into a sitting position, the seat totally engulfed by her enormous pink posterior, she paused for a moment, then oh-so-delicately placed her fat unwashed fingers, heavily stained with nicotine and closely resembling butcher's sausages, onto the keyboard. The dirty, bitten nails did not detract one iota from these magic writer's fingers, although at first glance one would undoubtedly surmise that the owner spent her life rooting about in gardening compost.

Like an acclaimed concert pianist about to embark upon a magnificent concerto, she took a deep breath and began to type furiously. The words flew across the screen, empty only moments before.

She had it now; she was in full flow. A series of minor belches passed unnoticed as she attacked the keys, and for the moment, the noise of her typing drowned out any further bodily eruptions.

The two mangy animals slept on in their hiding places, moving only to scratch now and then as fleas bit into them.

In her dirty, foul-smelling room, surrounded by rancid debris, fetid air and flea-ridden animals, the Muse once again perched upon the writer's shoulder as she sat at the keyboard with yet another cigarette dangling from the corner of her mouth. The ash dripped as ever unnoticed onto the disgusting pink robe.

All else was forgotten as she typed away like a woman possessed, regurgitating the salient points from her first book, and enlarging on the theories expounded therein. The cigarette burned down until it reached the dribble on her lips, sticking like glue to her mouth. She did not notice; her mind was working overtime.

In large print at the top of the page the authoress typed the words the world awaited with bated breath. This would be another masterpiece, from the expert herself. It would be even better than her first offering. Her word would become law across the globe. It could not fail. It would undoubtedly be another massive success.

Smiling lop-sidedly at her own brilliance as an authoress, and revealing black rotting teeth through the nicotine-stained lips, she took on the appearance of a malevolent gargoyle. Caring nought for her looks, her surroundings, or her animals, she continued to pound the keyboard as the words flowed through her fingers onto the screen.

The second definitive work from the mistress of her craft. Her legendary expertise would bring generations of readers to these books, seeking her advice.

She leered at the very thought, her chins wobbling as she pecked furiously at the keys. She would become the world's undisputed leading authority on the subject; a literary giant.

The rollers finally gave up the unequal struggle to stay

entangled in the dirty strands of hair and flopped unceremoniously into her lap, and thence onto the floor, totally ignored by the world-famous writer as she launched herself into her next blockbuster.

With her chair dangerously overloaded beneath her, she wobbled with excitement as the words of the title appeared on the screen in front of her:

LADY LAVINIA FARQUHARSON-SMYTHE'S
ESSENTIAL GUIDE TO ETIQUETTE AND
PERFECT MANNERS

VOLUME II